protecting his forever

The Forever Series - Book One

LeAnn Ashers

First Edition: 2016

Proof reader: Emma Mack www.ultraeditingco.com

Designer: Regina Wamba
Photographer: Wander Aguliar
Formatted by: Brenda Wright, Formatting Done Wright

dedication

To every woman that hasn't found their soul-mate.
Just know he/she is out there. So never settle for less
than what you deserve. Which is the world. <3

LeAnn Ashers

one

Looking around the clothing store, I can't shake the feeling of someone watching me. Shrugging my bag up higher on my shoulder, I walk around the rack of clothes just as a loud bang comes from behind me. Startled, I jump and turn around. A man stands a few feet away from me. I give him a kind smile then make my way over to the next rack. I look through the shirts trying to find my size when I see movement in my peripheral and notice the man is lurking close by. I scan the area nearby, taking notice of the tattoo that covers half of his face. It's a gang symbol, one I recognize from the graffiti that marks up half of the buildings on the West side of town. The look in his eyes is angry, hateful as he stares. Acknowledging his presence, I pass him an uneasy smile as I dip my head to my chest and set the shirt I was eyeing back on the rack. My senses are escalating, shouting DANGER! DANGER! DANGER!

I make my way toward the exit, taking casual strides as not to draw attention to myself. But once my feet pass the threshold of the store, I pick up the pace, hurrying to my car. Reaching into my purse, I clutch my phone in my hand then glance over my shoulder quickly. Shit! He's stepping off the sidewalk and heading in my direction.

Don't panic, Sydney. Calmly, I dial my brother's number.

"Hello?" My brother picks up on the third ring.

"Ethan, I'm being followed." I sound panicked even to my own ears.

"What? Where are you?" he shouts.

"Downtown at the new clothing store." I peek over my shoulder cautiously and see that the tattooed man is still following. Sucking in a sharp breath, I walk around my car and head back toward the store, knowing that stopping to get in my car isn't a good idea.

"What do I do, Ethan?" I whisper.

Three rough taps peck at my shoulder. My body stiffens. Gripping my phone tighter, I slowly turn around to face the man. "Gotcha!" He chuckles and makes a move toward me. His hands claw at me but I jump back and take off running. His heavy boots slap the ground behind me.

"Sydney!" Ethan yells into the phone just as fingers thread into my hair, and with a hard yank my head hits the concrete with a smack. My phone slips out of my hand from the impact and slides across the ground. Digging my heels into the asphalt, I attempt to push myself up to a standing position. He tightens his grip on my hair, dragging me across the ground between two cars.

I dig my nails into his large hands, tearing at his flesh as I squirm and pull with all my might. He grunts and loosens his hold on me for a split second before I rip my hair from his grip. Despite how painful it is, I'm loose. Tattered strands of hair fall to the ground.

Grabbing the handle of the car behind me, I lift myself up to my feet. Everything is a blur and dark spots cloud my vision. Chuckling brings me out of my stupor. My gaze shoots over to the man as he closes the distance between us.

"Feisty. I like it." His voice is husky and dark.

Fear rattles my chest and I try to take a step back, but his heavy fist lands across my face. Pain shoots up my jaw and through my mouth. My body sways. Stumbling, I fall to the ground, landing hard on my tail bone. His body lands on top of mine and pushes me down on my back. His legs go on either side of my waist, pinning me beneath him. His unforgiving knuckles pound at my chest, neck, and face. I pull my forearms up to protect myself instinctively, but it's no use, I'm a fragile doll compared to his strength. His assault is brutal and feels endless. Disoriented and helpless, I feel a deep lull from the blows to my head. He brings his fist back to deliver another ruthless blow, and bright crimson catches my eye. That's when I feel it—the sensation of blood trailing down my cheek.

Snap out of it, Sydney! Fight back!! My inner strength shouts at me, gaining my attention. My fight or flight instinct kicks in, and I inhale a painful breath and begin to kick, scratch, and punch anyway I can. I drill my fist into his junk then with all my might, I kick my knees up into his back. He falls to the side and shouts a slew of obscenities as he clutches himself, writhing in pain. His legs are still locked around my waist, but I'm free enough to lean forward. I jab my elbow into the side of his face then buck him off my body.

Quickly, I grip the hood of the car beside me and pull myself up off the ground, trying to catch my breath to call for help. *How the hell has nobody heard my attack?* My body aches with every inhale of breath, each stretch of a limb. His iron like hand clamps onto my calf, and in a panic I blindly kick my foot out. A loud crack followed by a husky scream pulls my attention down to my attacker. He releases my leg and cups his nose as blood flows freely between his knuckles. My escape within reach, I turn and run back towards the store.

My adrenaline courses through me at lightning speed. I don't watch for passing cars or bystanders as I approach safety. Rushing up to the sidewalk I take a backward glance to make sure my attacker isn't behind me when I stumble forward and my face smashes against something hard. Strong hands grip my shoulders and pull me up to my feet. I thrash my small fists forward, hoping to connect with my attacker. *How did he close in on me so quickly?* My breathing is labored, and I dart my head around wildly looking for the man. He pops around the side of the car and starts toward me. Jerking back, I try to dislodge the hands from my arms.

"Please!" my sob is broken and breathless.

I feel his warm breath against the shell of my ear as his grip tightens around me. "Sydney!"

Suddenly my feet are placed against the ground. When my eyes meet his, all the air seizes from my chest. His eyes are hard and devious, but not at me. I know this man. He's my brother's friend. He gently grabs my waist and thrusts me behind his body then charges at my attacker, forcing him to the ground. The attacker's head smashes against the pavement as his foot comes back and kicks against his skull.

The man makes a garbled sound as his body stills, but Kane's kicks continue. I know if Kane doesn't stop, he'll kill him.

"Stop!" I scream.

Much to my surprise, he stops. Sucking in a much needed breath, I crumble to the ground as shock consumes me. My whole entire body shakes uncontrollably, harsh sobs wracking through my chest. Clasping my hands together and wringing them tightly in an effort to control them. *Did that really just happen? To me?* Resting my elbows on my legs, I hold my head between my hands and try to comprehend what the hell just happened to me. Did I really just almost get kidnapped? Raped? Worse? Shaking my head in disbelief, I look over at my attacker lying on the ground.

"Are you okay?" a deep voice asks.

Looking up, I see Kane kneeling beside me. I nod yes

then hug my arms to my chest to hide my trembling hands. *I'm not okay, not at all.*

His hands tug at my chin until I'm looking up at him. His eyes are full of concern and I know he doesn't believe me. He takes off his shirt and presses it to the cut on my head and brushes the hair out of my face. His gentle care and concern snaps all the control I have left. A sob escapes and the dam breaks.

A second later I'm hit with his warmth. His arms wrap around me, and my face is pressed hard against his chest. He lifts me onto his lap with both arms wrapped around me tightly.

"Shhh, it's going to be okay. I've got you," his deep voice sooths. Relief washes over me knowing I've been saved, still the tears continue to fall.

The moment is interrupted by the sound of sirens blasting in the wind and tires screeching to a halt.

"Sydney!" My head shoots up at the sound of Ethan's voice. Climbing from Kane's lap, I run straight toward my brother and slam into his chest. He lifts me off the ground and holds me tight. I whimper in pain, and he places me back on the ground.

"You took a couple years off my life, Sydney! Don't ever fucking do that again, you hear me?" His stern voice makes me choke out a strangled laugh. *Delirious, obviously.*

He studies my face as he takes in my injuries, and suddenly his demeanor shifts and his eyes grow dark.

"What did that fucker do? He. Is. Dead," he grounds out between his teeth.

I look over at the man lying on the ground being handcuffed by an officer, and Ethan charges toward him.

"Stop, man!" Kane rushes over and pulls Ethan back.

"Kane?" my brother asks in shock as he shoves Kane's hand off his shoulder.

"Ethan, stop! He saved me!" I shout.

Kane confirms my words with a quick nod toward Ethan. He looks down at the attacker then back to me then to Kane, and he suddenly connects the dots. He pulls Kane into a one armed hug.

"Thank you, brother."

A hand clasps over my shoulder, and I shout as I jump back.

"Woah, Sydney! It's Chase." Chase thrusts his hands up, palm out. "It's just me! Calm down. You're safe now."

"I'm sorry, I'm just a little jumpy," I tell Chase guiltily.

"It's okay, baby girl." He gives me a sympathetic smile. "We need to get you checked out by the EMT." He motions over his shoulder to the two paramedics pulling a gurney from the back of their ambulance.

I nod my head slowly, then look up at Kane who is watching me intently. My adrenaline washes away like the sands on the shore. Suddenly the ground shifts and everything blurs. Gripping my head that feels like a two-ton weight, I fall to the ground not able to support my weight. "Sydney!" Ethan's voice sounds distant as it echoes through my mind. Heavy footfalls and shouting surround me, then hands wrap around my arms and legs, lifting me up off the ground. The pitch black solace of my mind pulls me deeper and deeper as the darkness cloaks me.

two

I wake with a groan, tugging the blanket higher under my neck as a shiver racks through my body. Hospitals are always so freaking cold. Before opening my eyes, I know where I am. The monitors beep in melody throughout the halls and the IV in my arm is another sure sign, as well as the smell of antiseptic that burns my nose. A door slams nearby. Startled, my eyes shoot open.

"You're awake," a deep, rough voice asks.

Looking over to the side of the bed, my eyes widen as they land on Kane.

"Kane..." I trail off, confused.

"That's me." He smirks and leans back in his chair with his hands folded behind his head. Rolling my eyes at him,

I tug at the blanket covering me.

"How are you feeling?"

"I'm sore. My head and face feels like they've been rolled over by a steam roller. I'm a little shook up, but I'll be okay." I sigh and reach down to grab the other blanket at my feet. It seems like I can't get warm.

"Let me get that." He places his hand on my shoulder and eases me back against the pillows. He takes the blanket at my feet and lays it over me and proceeds to tuck me in like a burrito and fusses over the pillows behind my head.

"What's that look for?" He holds an extra pillow in his hands.

"Oh, nothing." I bite my lip and try to contain my smile.

"I'm going to get the doctor and tell them you're awake." He walks out the door and closes it quietly behind him. As soon as it closes, the breath I didn't know I was holding blows out roughly. Yesterday was the first time I have ever met Kane. I've only seen him in photos with Ethan and Chase from their time in the military together. He showed up and saved me during the worst moment of my life. How or why, I'll never know. But beyond all, I'm grateful.

A scattered breath shakes my chest as I think about what happened to me yesterday, and a million different thoughts hit me at one time.

Who was the man who attacked me?

Why did he attack me?

Oh goodness, he could have raped me, kidnapped me, or worse—murdered me!

Will he come back for me?

Wiping the tears from my face, I wince as my hands rub over my broken and bruised skin. My hands fall to my lap, and I see blood. A sob escapes, and I place my hand over my lips to choke back the cries. A knot lodges in my throat, and it becomes harder and harder to breathe. Panicking, I grip my throat as black spots cloud my vision, smacking my hands against the hand rail.

Please someone help me!

I can't breathe. I heave and wheeze as I suck air into my oxygen deprived body.

"Sydney!" Hands touch my face, and I hear voices yelling as they enter the room. The fog is too thick, too heavy to get through. I close my eyes, and then I feel myself fall.

"Sydney, can you hear me?"

"Hm?" I mumble while turning over and snuggling deeper into bed.

"Wake up for me, sweetheart. Let me see those beautiful eyes."

Cracking one tired and sore eye open, Kane's face is the first thing I see. His hands gently caress my face.

"How are you feeling?" He tucks a piece of hair behind my ear that has fallen on my face.

Hitching the blanket higher up under my neck before I

answer, I say, "I'm okay." It comes out as a raspy whisper. "Your mom just left. You've been out two whole days. The doctor said your body must have fallen into complete shock because you wouldn't wake up, and that it's common for victims who have experienced trauma such as you have. Your brain kinda takes over and shuts everything down to let you rest. It scared us all. Hell..." He sighs and rubs a rough hand over his face while looking up at the ceiling.

Two days? I pull my exhausted and sore body up and look around the room. Shaking my head to clear it, I mutter, "I'm sorry. Everything must have hit me all at once. Have you been here this entire time?"

With a curt nod, he rests his hand on the bed. Taken aback by his presence all this time, I grasp his hand and give it a squeeze. He smiles broadly, and I immediately blush, diverting my eyes to his hand laid in mine. There are visible scars all along his rough and cracked skin which are marked with callouses.

"It's understandable, you've been through a lot. But you're safe now." His hands curls around mine and our fingers intertwine. Giving him a small smile, I look up at him through my eyelashes. He doesn't mention why he's stayed with me since I've been in the hospital, but I figure he has his reasons and while I'd like to understand why, my brain is too cloudy to comprehend much more.

"Thank you for saving me. I don't know what would have happened if you didn't show up. I was trying to go for help, but he was so close behind..." I trail off as a sob escapes. The emotions are just too thick to grasp.

"Sweetheart, it's something *any* man would do. That fucker deserves hell of a lot more than jail," he growls out the last part.

"I'm sorry you have been stuck here the past few days."

"There is nowhere else I want to be," he answers honestly as he strokes my cheek bone.

"Ouch!" I hiss out as the doctor probes all of my cuts and bruises.

"Watch it!" Kane growls and pushes the doctor's hand away.

"Well, I see that you're fine." The doctor coughs nervously and backs away from Kane. "Change your bandages twice a day. I'm writing a prescription for some ointment to put on your cuts."

I thank him and he leaves the room.

As soon as the door closes, I say, "Well that went well."

Kane glares at me and paces the room.

"What are you still doing here? I'm sorry if this comes out rude but I'm curious." I arch my eyebrow.

"Your mom wanted someone to be here in case you woke up, and I wanted to make sure you were okay." He answers simply.

"So for the last forty-eight hours you've halted your life just to play chivalrous hero? Do that often, Kane?"

He shoots me a warning glare, so I probe no further. I am, however, growing frustrated with his overbearing protectiveness. Hell, I'm in the hospital with twenty-four-hour staff monitoring me. My attacker is in jail—or so Kane says. So why is he still here? My frustration mounts, but I keep my tongue in check and bite down on my lip to stop myself from saying something I probably don't mean. *Do I?* Ugh, this damn fog! I just need to clear my head. I throw back the covers and place my feet on the ground. I need to get out of this bed, out of this room. It feels like the walls are closing in on me, and Kane's pacing is doing nothing to help my frayed nerves.

"Where do you think you're going?" Kane stomps over to me and tries to settle me back against the bed.

Smacking his hands away, I hiss at him, "I have to pee!" With something to prove, I stand too quickly and my world sways as I tip to the side.

"See!" he grounds out between his teeth as he locks his hands around my waist and catches me before I hit the floor. He lifts me off the ground bridal style.

Sighing, I admit, "I just got out of bed too quick."

Peeking up at him, I'm hit with how unbelievably gorgeous he is. He is rugged and has the look about him that is all man. He is over a foot taller than me. Little scars cover his neck and chest. He has two full sleeves and it's sexier than hell. I may or may not have a thing for a guy that has that bad boy look. He catches me looking, and smirks, causing me to blush.

He shakes his head no and puts me back into bed, then

presses the button to call the nurse. I huff and sit back in bed with my arms crossed across my chest while glaring at Kane. Who does he think he is? If I want to pee by myself, I will go pee!

"Did you need something, honey?" the nurse asks as she enters the room.

"A shower and to pee."

"Of course! Follow me," she says and waves me out of bed as she turns on her heels.

Kane's husky voice stops her. "She needs assistance. She tried to get out of bed on her own and almost fell."

"Oh, of course. I will help her." She rubs her hands nervously. Her eyes dart between Kane and me as she makes her way to the bedside.

Rolling my eyes, I push my feet back over the side of the bed. My body protests with every movement. The nurse wraps her hand around my bicep and leads me to the bathroom. I can feel Kane's gaze watching my every moment.

The nurse walks inside with me and shuts the door. I stand there awkwardly. I don't need help. This may be her job to help people with things like this, but it makes me very uncomfortable. She turns on the shower and motions for me to step forward.

I push my hand toward her and with too much attitude that isn't necessary, I bark out, "I can do this myself. That man out there is being too protective. I'm not even sure what he's even doing here."

She smiles knowingly and motions to the string next to

the shower. "It's okay, honey. I think he's being kinda sweet, but I understand how you feel. If you need help, just pull that string and I'll be right in, if he doesn't rescue you first." She winks with a bubbly grin.

As soon as she leaves, I all but rip the hospital gown off my body, not even checking the water before I jump into the shower. The cold water soon turns hot and kneads at my sore muscles. Grabbing some hospital soap, I scrub my body raw. Hoping to scrub the memories of yesterday away.

Once my body is scoured clean with rough, red patches of heat and the entire room is filled with steam, I turn off the shower then wrap a towel around my chest. I step out onto the ceramic gray floor, slipping on a mist of water and fall directly onto my ass. The steam has dampened the floor like it was sprayed with Pam. Groaning, I grab my ass.

"Great, add a broken tail bone on top of this," I mutter to myself and push up to my feet.

A knock sounds at the door.

"You okay in there?" Kane asks.

"I'm just dandy, thank you!" I know I shouldn't be snippy with him. Although he's one of Ethan's closest friends, and I've heard a lot about him, that doesn't mean I know him from Adam.

I carefully step over to the bathroom mirror and take in my appearance. My lip is busted and swollen. Stitches knit the skin on my cheek together, little speckles of blood dotting the bruised flesh. There's a knot on my forehead, and my head throbs persistently. Seeing myself, I realize the injuries aren't nearly as bad as I expected. I'm banged up pretty good, but it could have been much worse. I'm lucky, that's for sure.

I towel off, careful of the tender bruises on my body. Looking around the room I notice that I didn't bring any clothes in with me. I peek my head out the door and look around the hospital room, no sight of Kane. Coast is clear. I step out of the bathroom and go to the small locker to see if by chance my mom may have left me some of my own clothes so I'm not dressing in one of those itchy gowns. A husky grunt from behind, startling me. I jump and turn around quickly, clutching the towel to my chest. My eyes trail up his hard and lean body, broad and tight chest, meeting flared nostrils and a pair of hooded, darkened eyes.

I cup my hand over my mouth with words caught in my throat. God only knows what kind of word vomit I may spew, and I've been edgy enough with this man today. I swallow back a gulp, "Kane?" my voice is barely a whisper.

He snaps out of it his fog-filled daze and thrusts a handful of clothes toward me without so much as a word. I take the clothes and look down at my old granny panties resting on top of the stack. Hundreds of Pooh Bears hugging honey pots cover the panties, and they're folded perfectly to reveal a visible hole on one of the butt cheeks. *Fuck my life.*

Palming my face, I groan out loud. Kane looks down at me with a mischievous smirk playing at the corner of his mouth, a low chuckle rumbling through his chest as his shoulders visibly shake. Giving him a death glare, I clutch the clothes to my chest and step around him to make my way back to the bathroom.

"Nice panties," he calls over his shoulder.

"Ha-ha-ha, laugh it up." Turning around I flip him the bird over my shoulder and slam the door closed.

Holy shit. I'm going to murder my mom. Why did she bring my old panties from middle school? I toss the clothes on the counter and drop the towel to the floor. Searching through the pile for my bra, I find that she hid my regular panties under my shirt. *Thanks, Mom.*

An hour later, she shows her cheeky face. Crossing my arms over my chest, I give her a death glare. Kane chuckles at me, so I turn my glare toward him instead.

"Honey, I'm glad to see you're awake," she gushes and walks over to give me a hug. Closing my eyes, I hug her back tightly, basking in her loving hug.

She lets go and touches my face gently, smoothing my hair back. Her kind face is etched in concern. Tears come to her eyes. "You scared me," she whispers.

"I'm sorry, Mom." I rub her hand.

"I know, honey. Some deranged man tried to hurt my little baby." Her bottom lip trembles as her eyes fill with tears. She blinks and one falls down her cheek. My heart breaks that she had to go through this. Lifting my arms, I motion her over for a hug.

Looking over her shoulder at Kane, he gives me a sad smile. Ethan and Chase stand by the door.

"Mom, I'm fine. That man is in jail and seems like he will be for a while." Kane told me earlier that the man had multiple warrants. One charge had me ready to throw up: rape and murder of a young woman about my age. That could have been me. Oddly enough, the girl's description matched mine: dark green eyes, long brown hair, short curvy figure.

One Month Later

Waking up to the sound of knocking at the front door, I panic and fall down onto the floor clasping my pounding heart. My eyes shoot to the clock on the nightstand 10:00 AM. Letting out a deep breath I climb to my feet. My first thought when I hear the knocking is that the man has found me. *Come on, Sydney, if it was him, he sure as heck wouldn't knock on the door and he is in jail.* Before I reach the front door, the loud banging begins again.

Peeking out the peep hole, I see just the top of red hair. *Weird, who could this be?* Taser at the ready, I open the door. Something hard collides with my body and makes me a take a couple steps back.

Pushing the person off of me, I look to see who it is. Gasping, I squeak, "Brae?"

"In the flesh," she answers guiltily.

"Where the hell have you been?" I can't contain my temper. Brae was my best friend. Since the first day of college we had been inseparable. We went to a party after finals our senior year because we wanted to celebrate. I was busy dodging my stalker. Stalker may have been too strong of a word, but it seemed like he was always there every time I went somewhere outside of my apartment. Braelyn was talking to a guy, and when I left the room I never saw her again. I searched for her everywhere. I haven't seen her since.

"I, uhh. It's a long story." Tears rush to her eyes. The Braelyn I know is tough and doesn't cry. Something horrible has happened. Braelyn had a horrible life growing up at the hands of her stepfather. He was abusive and her mom sat there and watched, but that only seemed to make her stronger. This girl standing in front of me with her eyes overflowing with tears has been broken by something much worse.

"We have plenty of time. Let's get you fed." I lead her into the kitchen, her small, fragile hand in mine. Her wrist is really small, smaller than what would be considered normal.

I watch as she lifts her small frame onto the stool, her hands shaking as she pushes her hair out of her face. Her cheeks are sunken in, her lips chapped, stains are covering her clothes and her hair needs a good wash. Bones are sticking out of her chest. She is starving.

Turning around, I don't want her to see my tears. Braelyn doesn't deserve this shitty hand that has been dealt to her. Taking a glass out of the cabinet, I fill it to the top with water and hand her a banana.

From the corner of my eye, I watch as she shakily peels the banana back and eats half of it with one bite. Tears fall down my face that I don't try to hide. *Braelyn, what has happened to you?*

Fixing her two sandwiches, I place the plate in front of her. She takes one sandwich off the plate and crams it in. If she doesn't slow down, she will get sick. "Slowly," I tell her softly, my hand resting on her arm.

She nods and slowly takes a bite. My heart is breaking for this girl. She finishes the first one and then before she can get to the second she jumps up and runs to the bathroom. Her body is reacting to not having food for a long time.

I follow behind her. Taking a washcloth out of the linen closet, I wet it and hand it to her. Her eyes search my face. Reluctantly, she takes the cloth from me to clean herself up.

"I was starving, Sydney," she says with a hitch in her voice.

"I know, Braelyn," I confirm and hand her an unopened tooth brush from under the sink. "I will be in the kitchen. I think we need to talk."

She nods her head, and I rub her back soothingly. Walking to the living room, I sit down on the couch.

She comes in a few minutes later and stops at the end of the couch, twisting the bottom of her shirt nervously.

"Come sit down, Braelyn." I pat the seat beside me.

She walks over and sits down, tucking her feet under her. Before I can say anything, she starts to talk, "Remember the party we went to at the end of finals?" Nodding my head, she continues, "I was hanging with this guy. He was sweet—too sweet. He offered to get me a drink, and I immediately agreed. Never once did I think that he could have put something in it. Thirty minutes or so later, I was getting dizzy, and my vision was blurred. I ran off into the woods.

I remember falling down, and I could feel footsteps coming toward me. I couldn't move, my arms and legs felt like lead. Then I heard a rip and my clothes were torn off my body."

She stops and looks directly at me. "He raped me and took the only thing I had left of my innocence. This man destroyed me. I ran and never looked back. I've been homeless." Her face crumples, and I take her into my arms as she sobs into my neck.

"Honey, everything is going to be okay now. You will stay here with me." I rub her back and hold her closer to me. She is my sister. We may not be blood, but I love her just the same. Tears fall down my face, hurting for her.

"That's not all," she says into my neck. Rearing back, I wait for her to finish. "Two days ago the same man that raped me found me." She pauses and wipes the tears from her face with her sleeve. Sucking in a sharp breath, I hold her tighter.

"He tried to again, but I fought him off and ran. I knew the only place I could go is here. I'm afraid that I've put you in danger." Her bottom lip trembles.

"Let me call my brother, he is a cop," I tell her and grab my phone. Standing, I walk into the kitchen, leaving Brae alone in the living room.

Dialing my brother, he picks up on the fifth ring. "Sydney?"

"Hey, Ethan, can you come over? I need to talk to you; I have a situation..." I trail off biting my lip nervously. I'm scared for Brae and for myself. How could I not be? The man that has hurt her is crazy.

"What?" he hisses.

Sighing, I say, "Just come over." I hang up and walk over to Brae who is clutching a pillow to herself.

"My brother will be here soon," I reassure her. She nods and stares blankly at the wall. Not knowing what to do, I slowly walk over to her wanting somehow to take away her pain. Seeing this man, no doubt brought everything that happened to her back to the surface.

"You want to take a shower?" I ask her hesitantly not wanting her to get embarrassed. She nods and stands up. Leading her to the shower in my room, I give her a fresh razor and tell her she can use my products. Turning around, I start to leave but her hand on my arm stops me.

"Thank you, Sydney." She gives me a small smile. Nodding my head, I grin at her.

"Go shower. I'll be downstairs," I tell her as I set some

clothes on the counter. Ethan will be here any minute.

I pace in front of the door impatiently. Two loud trucks roar up my driveway. Ethan is obviously in the red truck, but there's a black truck I don't recognize. My brother gets out and turns to the man in the black truck as the door opens. *Kane?* My eyes widen in confusion.

Stepping out onto the porch, I close the door behind me. Ethan and Kane are speaking in lower whispers and when Kane realizes I'm close by he pauses and cocks a brow up at my brother. He stalks towards me and my breath catches in my throat as my eyes connect with his icy blues.

The closer he gets, the more his face hardens. Confused, I look over at my brother who is staring at Kane like he has grown two heads. He climbs up the steps and goes to stand directly in front of me.

"You've been crying," he says bluntly, looking down at me.

"I-I-" I stutter and look at my brother who has now joined us.

"Sydney, what happened?" Ethan says, concerned and places a hand on my shoulder.

"My friend is in danger."

"Your friend?" Kane asks and looks at Ethan.

"She will explain," I tell them and walk into the house knowing they will follow.

"What are you doing here?" Ethan asks Kane behind me. Kane doesn't answer. I'm curious myself.

Why is *he here?* I haven't seen him since I left the hospital. Kane saved me and that is something I will never

ever forget. That day still haunts me. I got away from that man, but he was close behind. I know that he would have gotten me one way or another. Police would have been too far away. That man obviously didn't care about an audience or getting caught because he beat me and tried to kidnap me in broad daylight.

A creak of a floorboard on the steps brings me out of my thoughts. Glancing up, I see Brae slowly walking down the stairs looking down at us all. Stepping forward, I hope my face expresses that everything will be okay.

She timidly walks beside me. She looks at the ground, her whole body shaking. Kane and Ethan are a little scary—they're really tall, tattooed, and intimidating.

"Braelyn, this is Ethan, my brother." I motion to Ethan to step forward. He doesn't take his eyes off of her. He searches her over, assessing. Looking up at Kane, I find him staring at me. Blushing, I look away quickly.

"And this is Kane, my brother's best friend." Her eyes shoot up to look at him and then back to the ground. She is so freaking scared. Ethan looks at me and gives me a desperate look. My brother, raised by a single mom, has a soft spot for women. "She's scared," I mouth to him.

Taking her hand, I lead her to the couch and sit directly beside her. Feeling a presence sitting on the couch arm, I look up. Kane is sitting there just watching me like before. Shuddering, I turn my attention back to Brae. My brother sits right beside her, and Braelyn sinks into herself a little more.

"Braelyn, honey, I know this hard, but you have to tell

him. He is a police officer," I tell her softly while putting my arm around her.

Braelyn sighs sharply as she looks at Ethan. He inhales a large puff of air and repositions himself on the couch, looking in my direction. Braelyn flinches at his sudden movement and drops her eyes to the floor. Their exchange is different, and I notice Ethan is studying her face closely.

Then it clicks. Brae has the most beautiful eyes. They aren't one color—one minute they look blue, but they rapidly change with her mood. Braelyn is absolutely beautiful, like beyond super model pretty. She used to tell me that her beauty held a curse and it made her life hell.

Ethan shoots me a questioning look, and I shake my head, silently dismissing him for now. He nods, then turns back to Braelyn and places his finger under her chin lifting her face up to meet his. "I'm not going to hurt you," he tells her intently. She nods slightly and she tells him everything.

It's not easier hearing it a second time. I'm just as horrified.

A familiar, warm hand touches my back then trails down my arm, linking our fingers together. I look up at Kane and notice the tortured look in his eyes. Giving him a small smile, I turn back to Brae and Ethan.

Ethan looks horrified, pissed even. His jaw is clenched and his hands are hard in fists against his legs. Brae is getting to the part about the man finding her again. My brother's eyes widen and his gaze shoots to mine, understanding.

Kane squeezes my hand, his palm warm. I look down at our interlocked hands, and I can't help but notice how his hand dwarfs my small one.

The room quiets and I look at Brae who is staring at the ground again. Ethan jumps off the couch pacing the floor. Letting out a deep breath he turns to her. "Why didn't you tell the police about him the first time?"

She shakes her head before answering, "I was scared and humiliated. I didn't want anyone to know what happened to me. I just ran. I ran away from it all. What good it did me."

"Sydney could be in danger because of this," he tells her.

"I know…" she trails off before getting off the couch and turning to me. "I'm so sorry, Sydney. I'm leaving now. Putting you in danger wasn't my intent. I just didn't know what to do." A sob escapes as she heads for the door.

Shocked, I turn to Ethan ready to kill his ass. He watches me, his face full of guilt and regret. *Dick.* Jerking my hand free from Kane's, I get up to stop her.

"Braelyn, my brother is a dick. You're staying here with me," I tell her while glaring at Ethan.

"No," Kane grounds out behind me. Shocked, I turn around ready to smack the shit out of him too.

"No?" I hiss.

"Yes, no. You'll be in danger." He stands and crosses his arms. My mouth falls down to the floor.

"Stay with me," I hear Ethan say.

What the heck? Brae looks just as confused as I am and also a little scared.

"You can stay in the apartment in the basement," he elaborates.

She turns to me, pleading with her eyes.

Sighing, I tell her, "You will be safer there. Ethan will protect you."

Ethan gives her a winning smile when she sighs and agrees.

"Okay—" I start, but Ethan cuts me off.

"I'll protect you with my life." He takes a step toward her.

Braelyn hesitates, then as if she senses a safety with Ethan, she nods and smiles sweetly at him.

I stand in my doorway as Ethan drives off with Braelyn after Kane parks in a different place so Ethan can leave. Once they are out of sight, I step back into the house and close the door. It bounces off something and I hear a grunt. My eyes widen and I gasp as I pull the door open. Kane is standing there holding his hand. Grimacing I move closer to get a better look at his hand.

"Are you okay?" I hesitantly touch his hand. Turning it over I inspect his fingers. Running my finger over his, he winces and jerks back.

"Oh my God! I'm so sorry. Do you need me to take you to the doctor?" I rush out quickly. Kane grimaces dramatically and clutches his hand to his chest. Way to go

Syd. You broke the man's hand.

"What do you need me to do?" I plead with him. Guilt swarms through me after all he did for you. You repay him back by breaking his hand in the door.

"You can go on a date with me this Friday night." His voice void of emotion but his eyes show his amusement.

"Huh?" I stare at him like he's grown two heads.

His injured thumb brushes over my cheek bone, and butterflies swarm my belly. Shuttering I bite my lip to control my reaction. "This Friday night, be ready. I'll be here to pick you up at 7," he tells me in a low voice and then steps away from me and down the steps.

I stand frozen in shock for a few seconds. Did he just play me? He just fucking played me!

"I'm going to kill you!" I yell after him.

He gives me a smirk and chuckles slightly. "You heard me, baby. Dress casual." He winks and climbs into his truck. My mouth opens and closes many times not knowing what to say. He starts his truck and is gone before I can refuse. *Holy hell.* Slapping my hand against my face, I walk into my house and collapse against my door.

Climbing out of my car, I hear my mother yell, "Oh, my baby!

"Hey, Mom." I walk up the steps. She all but runs toward me and tackles me into a hug. My mom is a hugger—big time. She grabs my cheeks and squishes them together. "You look so cute!"

"Thanks, but I'm still mad about the whole hospital incident," I huff and walk in the house. I catch her grin from the corner of my eye. I haven't left the house since I left the hospital. I wanted to be alone and my mom respected that.

My mom is unbelievably beautiful. She has dark brown hair, beautiful brown eyes, and freckles covering her nose and cheeks. My mom could pass as my sister. She had kids young—just barely eighteen when she had Ethan. We never knew our dad, and she won't talk about him no matter how much I beg. We didn't have much growing up, but we had each other and moved every six months until I was a freshman in high school when we finally made Raleigh, Texas our home.

She laughs as she leads me into the kitchen.

"Ha-ha, laugh it up, Mom."

"Oh come on, baby. That was a good prank." She gives me a huge smile before wiping her tears away.

"Yes, it was, Mom. Especially since Kane was the one that handed me my clothes." I scowl at her. She presses her lips together hard, and her whole face turns red trying to hold in her laugh.

"Just laugh, Mom, and get it over with." I sigh and sit down at the island.

The smell of fried food hits me. My belly growls in anticipation.

"Kane saw your Pooh Bear panties!" She points at me and bends over laughing.

"That sure didn't faze him, considering," I mutter under my breath.

"What?" she whispers and walks over to me.

"Nothing, Mom." I sigh and bang my head against the top of the island.

"Oh my God! Did Kane come see you? Come on, tell me!" she squeals and shakes my shoulder.

Raising up, I look up at her. "Yes, Mom. He asked me on a date. Wait, no. He *told* me to be ready at a certain time, and that was that."

"Good." She grins and turns around, piling food onto a serving plate.

"Good?" I repeat with an arched eyebrow.

"Honey, you're a stubborn woman and knowing you, you would have turned him down." She doesn't turn around, just continues piling food onto the plate.

She's right. I never date. Not that I don't want to, but the truth is that every single date I have been on has been a disaster. Most are too grabby, and the others I don't feel anything for at all. I've never even had a serious relationship.

Looking around the kitchen, I see an abnormal amount of food littering the kitchen. "Are you expecting company?"

"Your brother and some special guest is coming. Plus, Chase and..." She trails off to look at me.

"Kane." She wags her eyebrows at me.

"Mom, don't even start!" I point my finger at her. "It's not even like that."

"Sure, if you say so, baby." She winks and goes back to her task.

Throwing my hands up in frustration, I hop off the stool. Walking through the house, I take a moment to admire the décor. Her house is as country as it gets—solid wood with horse shoes everywhere. This house was in bad shape when we got here, but it was ours. Mom saved for years to settle down on a farm, and it took months to get everything fixed the way she wanted it.

Opening the screen door, I go to the barn where my mom's horse is. I remember the day she got this horse.

Ethan was coming home from his first deployment, and I was home on a break from college. His truck thundered up the driveway with a horse trailer on the back. Confused, I walked down the steps. My mom didn't care about anything but seeing her baby boy, and she ran off the porch and opened Ethan's door before he even shut the engine off. She pulled him out of the truck and gathered him into a hug, sobbing against his shoulder.

He looked over her head and spotted me. Grinning, he let mom go. I ran to him and jumped, wrapping my arms around his neck.

"Missed you, sis," he told me before setting me down on the ground.

"I missed you too, bubby." I wiped away my tears. I missed him so freaking much. We were always close—he was my big brother. I may have felt like killing him half of the time, but he was my best friend.

"I got you something," he told Mom with a grin.

"What do you mean?" she started to protest but stopped instantly when the horse trailer moved. She turned to look at it and then it hit her. Her eyes widened. Ethan grabbed her hand and led her to the back of the horse trailer.

"Ethan, what did you do?" she whispered.

He released her hand then opened the door and climbed up in the trailer. A second later he pulled a beautiful, buckskin horse behind him. The horse that my mom always wanted. She always took care of us and never got herself anything. She put us before everything.

"Oh, Ethan, you didn't." She all but ran to the horse. Running

her hands down its body, she admired it before laying her head on its neck while her other hand rubbed its back.

Ethan pulled me into a hug, and I glanced up at my big brother – both of us smiling. "Welcome home, Ethan."

Snapping back from the memory, I open the horse stall and pull Buck out. Yeah, she named her horse Buck. I pull myself up on Buck bareback. Kicking my feet slightly, Buck takes off in a trot.

Nothing is more freeing than riding a horse, and after the day I had, this is just what I need. We trot next to the fence that runs down the driveway. Clicking my feet again, she takes off in a run. Closing my eyes, I bask in the feeling of the hooves hitting the earth, the sun beating down on my head. Hearing a truck driving up beside me I open them in time for my eyes to meet Kane's.

"Let me grab a plate for you before the boys get in here and eat up all the food." Mom grabs a plate and starts piling it with an ungodly amount food that I'll never be able to eat.

"Mom, I got this." I go to grab the plate out of her hand.

"I know you do, sweetheart, but Momma likes to spoil you." She gives me puppy dog eyes and hands me the plate.

Walking to the dining room table, I start to dig in. Cramming my face, I feel a presence walk into the room. My body stiffens because I instantly know who it is. Not looking up, I see hands grip the chair directly in front of me and pull it out.

"Ma! What's for supper?" Ethan yells from the mud room. Jumping in my seat slightly, I look up and my eyes connect with Kane. Blushing, I jump up to go check on Braelyn.

"Ethan Blaine! Don't you yell at me. You're not too old for a good old butt busting by your momma," she yells at him. She comes around the corner and glares at him with her hand cocked up on her hip.

The screen door opens again and in walks Braelyn. My mother's eyes widen and a hand goes to her mouth as she takes in Brae's appearance. Braelyn is a ghost of the person she used to be. She used to have curves that any woman would have killed for. She is still beyond beautiful, but I'm deathly afraid the old Brae is gone, never to be found again.

"Braelyn?" my mother manages to choke out.

Braelyn looks up at my mother with a small smile and nods. Ethan looks between them both, lost. Braelyn used to spend every break from college with me, but it seemed like she couldn't come when my brother was home.

My mother takes a small step toward her, and Braelyn meets her the rest of the way. My mother laughs slightly and leans back, wiping her eyes. "Come on, let's get you fed. Go sit down, and I'll bring you a plate," she tells Brae before turning to Chase and Ethan. "You go get your own food in the kitchen."

Leading Brae, who is twisting the bottom of her shirt nervously, to the table, I pull out her chair and help her sit down. Her body feels so frail. Sitting down beside her, I feel Kane's eyes on me. Looking down at my lap, I try to hide my smile.

Dating is something I rarely do, but I'm going on a date with Kane this Friday night. *Holy shit.* The idea feels different than any other date I have ever been on because *Kane* is different. It feels different with *him.*

Grabbing my fork, I dig into my food. I'm not one of those girls that eats like a rabbit. I eat because I can. It's sad when a woman is afraid to eat in front of a man.

Ethan sets a plate in front of Brae and then hands her a fork saying, "Eat." The old Brae would have ripped him a new asshole over his tone, but I watch as she just nods and eats her food slowly. A wave of sadness washes over me at the girl before me. Ethan sits down beside Kane, and the chair sliding against the hardwood floors causes Brae to stiffen tensely. Ethan gives her a silent, reassuring look, and slowly, her shoulders relax and she continues eating.

Finished with my food, I push back in my chair to stand when a hand stops me. "I got it, sweetheart," Kane says from behind me. He takes the plate from my hand and takes it in the kitchen.

Ethan clears his throat, and I slowly look over at him nervously. Ethan never let me date anyone when he was around. He always found something wrong with the guy and made his life hell until the guy canceled.

He arches his eyes brow at me and looks up glaring as Kane comes back into the dining room. I can't resist looking at Kane. To my surprise, he is smirking at Ethan with a look of determination. *Oh, yeah. Ethan isn't scaring him away that easy.*

I'm not a crazy person, and resisting Kane would be absolutely stupid. Kane is hot. The kind of hot that makes a woman combust with the smirk he has and that freaking dimple. *Hell.*

"You want some more pie, Chase?"

Chase gives her his panty-dropping smile that has her blushing.

"You can have all my pie you want," she says then her eyes widen as she realizes what she just said.

"Ma!" I hiss and drop my head to the table.

"Fucking-A, Mom! Don't say shit like that," Ethan yells.

Chase and Kane laugh their butts off. When I hear a soft giggle beside me, I look up to see Brae with a grin on her face. She notices Ethan and me looking at her and instantly drops her expression.

Taking my phone out of my pocket I check the time. Its eight p.m. and I need to go home and write. Pushing my chair back, I stand up and look at my mom. "I have to go." I walk over and give her a kiss on the cheek.

Early Friday Morning

As I leave the mall I get a sense of déjà vu. Gulping I try to block out the images of my attack. The hair on the back of my neck stands up the closer I get to my car. Letting out a deep breath, I quicken my steps.

The sight of a something sticking out of my windshield wipers has me stopping in my tracks. What the hell? I look at my surroundings before I continue closer to my car. Tugging my purse higher on my shoulder I grab the letter.

With shaky feelings I open it. The blood immediately drains from my face? Could this be an accident? The letter has just three words, and the message has me frozen in fear.

Found you Bitch.

Fisting the letter in my hand, I stuff it in my purse not wanting to admit that this could have been for me. Unlocking the door, I climb in the car and start the ignition then drop it in gear. I pull out of the parking lot quickly, not knowing that a man was sitting in his car a few feet away watching me.

Friday night

Tonight I'm going on a date with Kane. Butterflies swarm around my belly in anticipation. Slipping on a pair of black skinny jeans, I pair them with a maroon, mid-sleeve, flowy shirt. Wearing heels isn't an option. Taking the big barrel curling iron, I curl my hair into sexy waves. I line my eyes with liner and mascara and then I'm finished.

Stepping back, I admire myself. My curvy hips and big butt are on display. Taking my bra straps, I perk my tits up. Grabbing some tinted lip balm, I dab some on my lips. The black eye liner makes my green eyes pop.

I'm not someone who likes to toot her own horn, but I look hot. Grinning at my own expression, I take my purse off the floor and slip my Kindle and phone inside. My Kindle is always with me—you never know when I can sneak in some time to read.

Walking into my living room, I tidy up the room nervously. Glancing at the clock on the wall, I notice the time. 6:49 p.m. Butterflies swarm once more. I'm nervous and this kind of nervous hasn't happened to me before.

Peeking at the clock again—6:50 p.m. Sighing, I start to

sit down on the couch when the doorbell rings. My head snaps up to look at the door. *I can do this, I can do this,* I chant to myself. Standing tall, I walk to the front door.

My hand is on the doorknob. Taking a deep breath, I swing the door open. There he is. I can't stop the grin that overtakes my face. He steps forward into the light more and offers me a bouquet of roses.

He has a sideways grin on his face. Taking the flowers from him, I put them up to my nose and sniff.

Looking up, my eyes connect with his. His eyes are such a piercing blue. My eyes drag down his body. His arms are huge and covered in tattoos. That is hotter than hell. He has the hot bad boy look going on that I'm a sucker for. His lips. *Oh my God.* They're the perfect Cupid 's bow that is made for kissing. My eyes go to the bulge in his pants. If he is that well-endowed not hard then, wow.

Someone clearing their throat has me looking up. He's chuckling with his arms crossed and giving me a look that says "gotcha". *Smug bastard.* Blushing I stumble back, saying, "I'm just going to put these in water."

Grabbing the vase, I place the pretty flowers in it. Hands grab my hips and lips graze my ear. I can feel his hot breath on my neck. I shiver.

"You ready to go, baby?" he whispers into my ear.

Nodding my head, I turn around to walk out the door. He takes my hand. Grabbing my shoes by the door I slip them on. I wish I could wear heels. I'm jealous of those women who can wear heels doing anything because when I try, I'm like a newborn foal. I'm pretty sure my ankles won't ever be the same again after the last time I wore them.

He takes my key from my other hand and locks the door. He takes my hand again and leads me to the truck. I feel giddy. It's like I'm a teenager who is going on her first date. It takes everything in me not to giggle and smile like a goon.

Kane opens the truck door, and I look up to the seat. He has got one of those big trucks that I would have to have a stool to get in. Sighing, I turn to look at him.

He gives me a confused look. "How in the world am I supposed to get up there? I don't have giant legs like you."

"Like this, sweetheart." He chuckles slightly. His hands wrap around my waist.

"Wait what are—" I squeal as he lifts me off the ground easily and places me in the seat.

I look at him shocked. "Wow…" I draw out. He just lifted me like I was a child. *Holy hell.*

He chuckles and shuts the door. My eyes follow him as he walks to the driver's side.

With a turn of the keys, the engine turns over and the seats vibrate as it roars. He switches gears and his muscles bulges and veins pop out on his tattooed skin.

I see him glance out of the corner of his eyes. Jumping in my seat, I hurry and look out of the window. He totally caught me ogling him, but to my defense have you seen the guy?

He pulls out onto the highway and drives toward town. *I wonder where he is taking me?* Taking my purse, I sit it on the seat beside me. I wring my hands on my lap nervously. I'm busting at the seams.

We sit in complete silence. It's not the kind of awkward silence that makes you want to bang your head against the window, but a comfortable silence. I watch as the lights of the town come into focus.

"What do you want to eat?"

Glancing over at him, I manage to say, "Umm, it doesn't matter."

"Just tell me what you want." He sighs as he comes to a red light.

"I don't care?"

"Sydney," he growls.

Which automatically makes me laugh. "Aren't you supposed to pick the place to eat?"

"Sydney!" he grounds out between his teeth as he looks over at me while we wait at the red light.

I laugh again at his expression.

"Enough fucking games, what do you want?" He looks over at me pointedly.

"It doesn't mat—" I start to say but stop again when I hear him growl again. "Okay, okay! I'll stop, but seriously, I am up for anything. I'm not picky. I'm satisfied with a burger."

I can feel his stare on the side of my face. Glancing out of the corner of my eye I can see a slight smile on his face. I glance out of the window trying to hide my own grin.

We pull up in front of an old diner. Unbuckling my seat belt, I start to open my door when Kane's hand on my arms stops me. "What?"

"Let me open your door. Sit still." He smiles and jumps out before I can argue.

He walks around the hood of the truck and opens my door. Clutching his hands around my waist, he lifts me down from the truck, my body sliding against his body as he places my feet on the ground.

He lets me go but laces our fingers together and leads me toward the diner. His large hand dwarfs mine; I can feel the raised scars covering his hand. My thumb is resting on one on the top of his hand. Involuntarily, I rub the scar.

I can feel his hot gaze on my face when he feels my thumb. Shuddering, I go to open the door to the diner. He stops me again and opens the door for me. Walking inside, I'm hit with the smell of greasy food that makes my stomach rumble. It's so loud it's embarrassing. I hope that he didn't hear that. Glancing at him, I peek to see if he noticed anything. He is smirking at me with an arched eyebrow.

Yeah, he heard that. Heat floods my cheeks. A large woman pops out from the door behind the counter. "Sit wherever, and I'll bring your menus."

Looking around the diner, I notice that they still have the 50's style decor with the black and white checkered floor, red seats, and glass windows that line the entire front of the building. The woman has on roller skates. I'm not sure how she can still use them because she looks old enough to be my grandmother.

Kane leads me to a booth toward the back of the room.

I let go of his hand to sit down in the booth, and I expect him to sit across from me because I sit right at the end, but he picks me up and sets me closer to the window.

I never expected him to sit next to me; his presence beside me is intimidating. It's not that I'm scared of him because something about Kane always makes me feel safe. Maybe it's because of the first time I met him? I have a feeling that it goes beyond that.

A menu sliding in front of me breaks me out of my thoughts. Looking up, I see the woman standing beside Kane.

"What would you like to drink?" she asks with notepad in hand.

"Water," Kane answers her first.

"The same," I tell her with a smile.

"Kane?" The old lady gasps.

My head shoots up, confused. She covers her mouth to catch the gasp that falls from her lips as her eyes fill with tears. Kane stares up at her. Confusion written over his face. *What the heck is going on? How does this woman know Kane? I look at Kane and back to the lady.*

"I haven't seen you since you were a kid. You moved away and we never saw you again," She tells him sadly. You can see the hurt written all over her face. Her hands white from clutching the waitress pad.

"Meredith?" He finally looks up when it dawns on him.

"Yes!" she yells and leans forward to wrap her arms round his neck. He hesitates for a second before wrapping his arms around her. Her eyes follow his movement before closing them. The pure pain written on her face as she sobs onto his shoulder.

Putting my hand on Kane's back to offer comfort. I don't understand how he could have known this woman? I didn't even know he used to live in this town. Sucking my lips into my mouth to stop the urge from asking questions. Questions that I'm dying to ask.

"Your mother worked here for years, and I watched you every single day while she worked. Then she never came back. I hunted for you, Kane, and never could track you guys down." She starts crying again.

"I remember you now." "His voice deep and ragged.

My mouth drops open, confused.

"You used to give me cookies," he tells her and a smile tugs at the corner of his lips but slips instantly. His eyes are full of pain. He looks down at the table trying to hide it. The pain I saw in his eyes for that split second is the kind of pain that eats away at you, and suddenly I feel sadness for Kane, wondering what he felt in that moment. I place my hand on his and lace our fingers together, then lay our joined hands in my lap. Butterflies swarm my belly just at the small interaction.

"I'm going to get your drinks," Meredith says while looking between us. As she rolls away she looks back at Kane like she's expecting him to bolt. Kane's mother took Kane and left without a word. It's understandable why she's scared.

Kane watches her walk away, and I watch him closely. Opening my mouth to speak, I think better of it as my mind draws a blank and close it instantly. What do I say to this?

He tugs our entwined hands into his lap and clears his throat. He looks at me briefly then down at our entwined hand and lets out a deep breath. I don't look away from him. I can't, I'm entranced by the sorrow that swims in his baby blues.

"When I was a kid, my mom got mixed up with the wrong man. He was a drug dealer and got her addicted. We never stayed in one place for too long. The hell they put me through dragging me from one place to another, the fighting, drinking…it was too much for a kid. She overdosed when I was fifteen and since I didn't have any other family, I lived on the streets until I joined the Marines. I wanted better for my life than what she had given me."

"When I was young my mom used to work here. Meredith watched me during my mom's shift. She would sit me down on the counter in the kitchen and sneak me cookies. This was before my mom was addicted to drugs. My mom used to a great mom. That was before…"

My heart aches for Kane. What little I know of him, I'd never imagined he was brought up in such a cruel world. Kane was dealt a dirty hand at life, but he didn't let that affect the man he's carved himself into today. He wanted more in life, so he made something of himself. That shows his true character. I know that there is a lot more to the story, but it's not my place to ask. If he wants me to know, he will tell me if and when he's ready. My heart hurts for this man. A tear trickles down my cheek, and Kane's face softens. His hand comes up and with the pad of his thumb he delicately wipes away my tears.

"Don't cry for me, Sydney. The Marines is where I found myself. I've seen a lot of terrible things in this world, but seeing small children living in shacks with no food, living amid violence and hate...it gave me something to live for. My life may not have been the best, but I knew I could make it better. Something most people don't even consider after having a hard upbringing. The Marines is where I found my family, my brothers. Ethan, Chase, and Isaac. The Marines taught me respect, honor and so much more. Most of all I found something worth living for. Protecting those I love." He looks over at me as he finished, his eyes showing his emotion that he won't voice.

Wow... This man? No words. What I thought I knew about him is changed drastically.

"I understand, but if you ever need to talk. I'm here." I put my other hand on his forearm. Sliding closer to him on the seat, I wrap my arms around Kane's belly. My face hits his chest. One of his hands holds the back of my head holding me to him and the other wraps around me tightly.

My eyes flutter, closed and I bask in the feeling of his arms. His scent comforts me. I feel protected. Those arms are something I always want around me. Kane has something about him that puts me completely at ease. He makes me feel protected and that nothing can touch me.

The moment is interrupted when Meredith comes back to take our order. Kane's arms ease off me, and I sit up in my seat. She looks between Kane and me with her eyebrows raised before a smile creeps over her face.

"Who's this?" She motions to me.

"I'm Sydney." Smiling at her, I look down at the menu at the burger selections.

"She's beautiful, Kane," she whispers to him.

"She's more than beautiful." A gasp shoots through me, and I look at Kane who's staring at me in a way that has me believing that he can see all the way down to my soul.

"Well, I'll be," Meredith says under her breath but my eyes don't leave Kane's. "What can I get you guys?"

Breaking my gaze from Kane's, I scan the menu again. "I'll just take a burger with all the fixings. Except mayo."

"I'll have the same," Kane answers next.

She writes everything down and rolls away. Kane turns to me. "Tell me about you."

"Not much to tell, really." I shrug, but judging by Kane's cocked up brow, my answer isn't enough. "My mom was a single parent who worked two jobs just to keep food on the table. We moved every six months, sometimes the bills were just too much or work was slow. Me and Ethan learned early not to make friends because we knew we wouldn't be staying in one place too long. Ethan was my best friend; I guess you could say. I was a loner, I closed myself off from the rest of world and lived in the fictional world of the books I would read." I pick at the hem of my shirt nervously. "Ethan joined the Marines when I was a senior. I kept to myself that year. College is where I found myself and learned to live. Well sort of." I laugh slightly and glance up at Kane who's staring at me intently. "I learned to get out of my shell. When I wasn't in class or studying, I would volunteer at the woman's shelter or the veteran's center. Now I'm an indie romance author," I laugh under my breath as his eyes widen at the romance part.

"You write sex?" His eyes widen waiting for my answer.

"The whole book isn't sex." Rolling my eyes at how cliché people are.

"No social life? No boyfriends, dating, or prom?" Kane asks.

Shaking my head, I blush. "I rarely dated. The few guys I did date, I'd learn early on they weren't the right guy for me. No point in wasting my time on someone I felt nothing for. Ethan was always very protective of me in high school, so he scared them away."

"Good," he mumbles.

"Hey!" I smack him on the shoulder. "I heard that."

He just shrugs his shoulders and smirks at me cockily.

"Remind me to thank your brother the next time I see him."

"Oh, you think I didn't date in college?" I tease him. His smile drops.

Meredith brings our food to the table. My burger is huge, like the size of the small plate. I thank her as I lift the burger off the plate. Opening my mouth, I manage to get a small bite in, groaning at the taste.

"Shit," Kane hisses from beside me. Glancing out of the corner of my eye I see Kane staring at me with hooded eyes. He shifts uncomfortably in his seat. Setting the burger back on the plate, I turn toward the window to hide my laugh.

We finish our food in silence, but my eyes keep wandering back to the noticeable bulge in his pants.

While Kane pays for our food, I walk outside. The warm Texas air hits me. Closing my eyes, I bask in the feeling. My eyes shoot open at the sound of something coming from the alley. Walking toward it, I see an old man in dirty and ripped clothing. He's leaning with his head back against the wall. His hat says that he's a Vietnam vet.

Walking over to him, I bend down so I'm eye level with him. His body stiffens when I sit close to him, but he doesn't look up.

"Sir," I start but instantly jump when he sits up and we almost butt heads.

"I'm sorry," he says and then scoots back closer to the wall.

"Are you a vet?" I sit down on the ground in front of him. The scent of urine hits me, and I put my hand over my mouth to cover up my gagging.

"Yes, ma'am. A Vietnam vet." He smiles at me proudly. His face is weathered.

"Thank you for your service." I offer my hand for him to shake. He stares at for a second before putting his hand in mine. "Are you hungry?"

He jerks his hand from mine and looks at the ground. *Pride.* No matter what circumstances have put this man where he today, his honor and pride are things that can never be taken from him. Not waiting for an answer, I get up.

"I'll be back in a minute," I tell him over my shoulder. As I turn the corner to go back into the diner, Kane walks out looking around wildly.

"What's the matter?" I ask him when I'm right beside him.

"Sydney," he grounds out and grabs my hand.

"Wait, I need to go back inside." I jerk my hand from his and walk back inside. Spotting Meredith still at the counter, I walk over to her. "I would like to order two burgers, and a large order of fries. If you have bottled water, that would be great too. This is to-go."

"This will be 15.60," she says after she adds everything up on the cash register. Taking my card out, I pay for the food.

"Thank you. I'll put the food in now and it should be done soon," she says before heading into the kitchen.

"Expecting to get hungry later?" Kane chuckles from behind me. Giggling, I shake my head no.

"You should have let me pay for that."

Shaking my head again, I narrow my eyes at him. No way am I letting him pay for that. From the corner of my eye I see him shake his head in frustration. He's such a guy. Rolling my eyes, I lean back against the counter, watching through the little window into the kitchen at the man fixing the food.

Kane wraps his arm around me and hugs me into his side before whispering into my ear, "What were you doing over by the side of a building?"

Leaning the back of my head against his chest, I tell him, "I was talking to a friend."

"A friend?" I can hear the confusion in his voice.

I nod. To be honest, I'm sad. A person who fought for this country is living on the streets. Without food or water. Nothing. A man who served this country deserves to always have a place to sleep. Shame is what I feel.

Spotting a napkin on the counter, I take a pen from the cup by the register and jot my number down. If he ever needs anything I will help him. No questions asked.

"Here you go, honey."

Looking up I see Meredith holding a massive carry-out box and two waters. Smiling at her, I mutter a thank you before taking it from her.

"Here, let me take it from you."

I start to argue, but Kane already has it in his hand. Taking the waters, Kane puts his other hand on my back and leads us out of the diner.

"Wait. This way," I tell Kane as he tries to lead me toward the truck. He looks confused but follows me.

Walking into the alley, I see the man still sitting there. He looks up as I walk up beside him and then snaps his gaze to Kane who is standing behind me.

"I brought you something," I tell the vet and set the waters down beside him. Taking the food from Kane I bend down and hand him the tray of food.

"Here is two burgers and fries." His hands shake and his eyes never once leave the food. I almost choke up, but I hold it in. Grabbing the napkin from my back pocket, I hand it to him.

"If you ever need anything at all, let me know. Here's my number." He smiles and nods at me.

Stepping back, I look up at Kane who I can feel is starting at me with mixed emotions. Taking his hand, I lead him out of the alley and straight to his truck, not wanting the veteran to see my emotions.

Sadness sweeps through me. I worked at the veteran's center. Seeing someone on the streets, hungry and especially a veteran is like a punch to the gut. What if that was my brother? Blinking rapidly, I try to stop my tears. How can life be so cruel? How can people be so cruel?

Kane opens the passenger door before his hand goes under my chin and lifts so I'm looking up at him.

"That was the most amazing thing I ever seen, Sydney, what you just did." His face shows his raw emotion mixed with awe. Blushing, I watch as his eyes travel down to my lips. My lips part on their own accord. My heart races in anticipation. Is he going to do what I think he is? My hands grip Kane's biceps. My breathing comes out in shallow bursts.

He lifts me off the ground and onto the seat. I let out a squeal as I bounce on the seat for a second, and I place my hands on his shoulders to steady myself. His hand goes to my jaw before he presses a kiss to my lips. Without hesitation, my lips part, and I deepen the kiss. I slide my hands down his back, pulling him closer to me as I wrap my legs around his waist. My heart is beating out of my chest. Kane's warm lips caressing mine in a way that makes all the other kisses I've had fly out of the window. This kiss is a one-of-a-kind kiss that makes the world stop. Pigs fly. The kind of kiss that you will compare all others to.

He breaks the kiss a second later and lays his head on my shoulder trying to catch his breath. He presses one last kiss to my bare shoulder blade. Goosebumps break out across my skin. Holy crap! I close my eyes, trying to compose myself. It's taking everything in me not to jump his bones. That kiss. Minutes, seconds, I don't know, my breathing finally returns to normal.

My hands slide down his back seductively not able to help myself. At my movement Kane pushes himself off of me. My legs stopping him from moving farther back. Amusement showing on his face at my reaction. Scrunching my nose at him, I can't resist the urge to press one last kiss on his lips.

Unwinding my legs, I turn around in my seat so he can shut my door. Once it closes, I hold my hand to my face. *Holy monkey balls. Wow.* When did you grow a pair Sydney? Giggling I hold my face which is now burning with embarrassment.

He opens his door and starts chuckling when he sees my expression. *Jerk.*

"Come here, sweetheart." He motions for me to scoot over. Setting my purse on the other side of me, I slide over to the middle seat. His hand goes to my lap and curls around my leg. Heat shoots to my nether regions at the closeness of his hand. *Breathe, Sydney.*

I've never been touched there by anyone else but me.

With Kane's hand on my leg and the warm Texas air flowing through the cab as we head to my house, everything feels right in this world.

Six

Twenty minutes later, we pull up in front of my house. Grabbing my purse, I dig through it to find my keys. Kane jumps out and pulls me out of his door. Smiling, I bite my lip as he lifts me down. His hand goes to my back as he escorts me to my front door.

Unlocking my door, I turn to Kane. I really don't want this night to end. Nervously, I ask,

"Would you like to come in?"

"Sure, sweetheart." He smiles and leans forward. Closing my eyes, I prepare for the kiss.

Raising up slightly on my toes, the sound of the door opening has me popping one eye open.

"What are you doing?" Kane chuckles.

"Meanie." I smack his chest and walk into my house.

"Want to watch a movie?" I motion toward the stack of DVDs.

"Sure." He sits down on the couch.

"I'm going to change into my jammies, and I'll be back." Walking up the steps, I go to my room. Spotting some grey sweats on top of the dresser, I sit on the bed to pull off my skinny jeans. Lifting my top over my head, I grab Ethan's old Marines shirt and slip it on before walking back downstairs.

Kane looks up as I walk down the stairs. Smiling, I tuck a piece of hair behind my ears. "What do you want to watch?"

He shrugs his shoulders before answering, "I don't care."

Going to the DVDs, I pick up a new scary movie that just released. Showing it to him, I ask, "Is this okay?" He nods his head.

Popping it into the player, I grab the remote. When I turn around, Kane is still looking at me. Nervousness pits at the bottom of my stomach.

Shuffling to the couch, I sit on the other end of it. His arm is resting on the back of the couch. He stares at me with an amused expression. Shrugging my shoulders, I settle farther into my seat.

"Baby, get your ass over here." He smirks at me.

Crossing my arms across my shoulders, I lean farther back into my side of the couch. "Sydney?"

"Yes, Kane,"

"Over here, or I'm coming to get you."

Shaking my head, no, I pull my feet up under me. My eyes never leave Kane. In a blink of an eye, he is standing up and walking over to me. Gulping, I press my back to the back of the couch.

He wedges his arms under my knees and behind my back, lifting me up before he sits down in my spot with me in his lap.

One arm wrapped around me and one resting on my leg, I stare up at him. My eyes wander to his lips. Looking down, I rest my head against his chest snuggling in. He wraps both arms around me holding me close.

I'm not used to his. I dated but this feel different. Him just holding me I am overcome with his smell, warmth, and the security his arms bring. Safe. Secure.

Kane

Sydney is sound asleep in my arms. She sank into me and never moved. Letting out a deep breath, I lean my head against the couch. I'm surprised she didn't run out of the diner with her tail on fire after hearing my story.

My life sucked, there's no other way to say it. Every day I came home from school and picked her lifeless body off the floor. With her lying in her own vomit, I expected her to be dead every time I got home.

I should have left, but it wasn't that simple. No matter what she did to me or what she *didn't* do, I still loved her. She was still my mother somewhere deep down inside of her.

Fifteen years old, I came home late from school. She was lying there with an empty needle beside her. I knew something was wrong instantly. I was used to seeing her like that, but something was different.

Her skin was pasty and her lips were blue. I touched her arm, and it was ice cold. Looking at her chest I saw no movement, and I knew that my mother was dead. I walked to a neighbor's house and called an ambulance, but I didn't wait for them. I didn't want to be a ward of the state, so I ran, and I lived on the streets until I was eighteen. I went to high school, lived in the baseball dug out for three years, and nobody knew. Enlisting in the Marines was the best thing that ever happened to me. I miss my mom even though she didn't care about me. The memories as a kid had me hanging out for the hope she wouldn't be like that again.

I tuck Sydney close to my chest and stand up, then carry her upstairs to bed. She weighs basically nothing in my arms—she's so fragile.

Spotting her clothes lying on the floor in one of the rooms, I walk into that one. Gently, I set her down on the bed and pull the covers over her. She stirs and her eyes open.

Leaning forward, I kiss her forehead and whisper in her ear, "Goodnight, baby."

Backing up, I move to go downstairs when her hand wraps around my forearm. "Stay." Her voice is a mere whisper.

"Sydney," I start to argue.

Her eyes open and she whispers, "Please."

Sighing, I nod my head before going to the other side of the bed. Unbuttoning my jeans, I strip down to my boxers. Sliding under the covers, she immediately moves over so her head is lying on my shoulder.

Her brown hair fans out behind her. My arm goes around her hugging her close. Her leg goes over one of mine so nothing is separating us.

"Goodnight, Kane."

"Goodnight, sweetheart." Kissing the top of her head, I fall into a deep sleep that I haven't had in years.

Sydney

Stretching my arms above my head, I notice a heavy weight pressing against my body. Cracking one tired eye open, I look down. Kane is lying on top of me. His head is lying on the crook of my neck. My legs are on either side of him. One arm is under my body and the other is wrapped on the other side my neck.

My hands go to his back—smooth and warm. Raising my hand slightly so only my nails are on his skin, I drag my nails up his back and deep into his hair. His head rolls to the side a little and his warm breath sends goosebumps down my arms and neck.

"Good morning," Kane murmurs before raising up on his elbows. His erection hits my clit when he raises up. Hissing, my head shoots back exposing my neck. Tilting my hips, he hits my clit again.

"Sydney," Kane chokes out. His body tense with need. Letting out a deep breath, I look at Kane. His eyes search my face before he tugs the bottom of my shirt up so my breasts are exposed.

He stares down at them for a second not moving. My hands move up to cover them up, feeling embarrassed.

"No, don't do that." He stops my hands and looks up at my face. "You're beautiful." His hands run over my belly and around the swell of my breasts. His mouth descends to my nipple and sucks deep.

"Oh God." My hands to go his head to hold him to me. The feeling shoots straight down to my pussy making me dripping wet.

His other hand slips into my sweats and his fingers trail my inner thigh. Shuddering, I wait in anticipation. He switches to one finger and trails it around my pussy, not touching my lips but close enough to drive me crazy.

"Do you want my fingers, baby?" he growls into my ear.

"God, yes." My hands go to his hand and I slam his mouth onto mine.

His fingers are on my lips now. Shifting my hips, I try to get him closer. His finger taps my clit and my legs squeeze him tighter. Moaning into his mouth, I dig my hand into his back.

"I got you, baby," he whispers against my lips before capturing my mouth in a kiss that has my toes curling.

His thumb circles my clit. Hissing, I pull him closer to me wanting more. Needing more. A finger slips into my pussy, and I clench around his finger at the intrusion. He gently pushes his finger in and out.

My breathing becomes rapid and labored. Throwing my head back, the burn in my belly intensifies. His finger curls and rubs this spot that has me crying out. His teeth clamp around my nipple and he bites slightly. My back arches off the bed as the powerful orgasm plows through me.

Collapsing onto the bed, I try to catch my breath. I can feel Kane looking at me. Blushing, I put my arms over my face. *Oh my God. Did that really just happen?*

"You're the most beautiful thing I have ever seen," he tells me softly as his hand rubs my cheek bone tenderly.

My eyes meet his, and I'm overcome with emotion. The way he is looking at me, it's like I'm his world. Closing my eyes, I lay my head back down on the bed. This is a dream. Stuff like this doesn't happen to me.

A bit of pain on my nipple has me yelping. Raising up on my elbows, I look down at Kane shocked. He just bit my nipple.

"No, you're not asleep." He chuckles before bending down to lick my aching nipple.

Grabbing the pillow beside my head, I hit him with it before climbing off the bed, pulling my shirt down as I go. Should I tell him I'm a twenty-four-year-old virgin? I have never considered giving that part of me to any man I've ever dated. This with Kane is different. This man could own every part of me.

He is lying on the bed with his elbow propped up, his head resting in his hand. His abs and tattoos are on display. God, he's sexy.

"You like what you see?"

Averting my wandering eyes that had settled on his noticeable erection trying to rip through his boxers, I can't help but blush.

"I, uhh. You're hot," I blurt out. "I'm going to go fix breakfast." I point toward the stairs.

Gripping the hand rail, I rush down the stairs and straight into the kitchen.

Reaching into the cupboards, I pull out all the ingredients for some pancakes. The stairs creak as Kane walks down. Grabbing a mixing bowl, I put all the ingredients in it.

I feel Kane before I see him. He sweeps my hair off one shoulder and kisses my neck softly. Closing my eyes, I sink into him..

"Baby, let me do this."

"I got it."

His hand stops me and takes the spoon from me. "Go relax." He smacks me hard on the ass and pushes me gently to the side.

"Kane," I huff and try to take the spoon back.

"No, let me do this." He puckers his lip out and gives me those puppy dog eyes. I don't bother to tell him how ridiculous he looks.

"Fine." I go to the other end of the island and sit on the stool.

He concentrates as he mixes everything that I had measured out. His arm muscles bulge as he stirs. My eyes never leave him.

"You're staring," he tells me as he turns on the stove.

"Yep," I answer honestly.

He grins at me over his shoulder. Smiling back, I tuck a piece of hair behind my ear.

We cuddle on the couch for a couple hours, full from breakfast. His hand is running through my hair making me sleepy. I have never felt so relaxed.

"I have to go, baby." He kisses me on the temple before lifting me off his lap and setting me down onto my feet in front of him.

"Okay," I tell him, disappointed.

"I'll be back." His eyes search my face and his hands push deep into my hair. Tugging at the strands he pulls my head back. Biting my lip, I stand up on my tiptoes and wrap my arms around his neck. His lips meet mine in a searing kiss.

"Goodbye, Kane." I give him another quick kiss as he sets me back down to my feet.

"Bye, sweetheart."

He walks over to the door and slips on his shoes. Walking over, I stand by him. Opening the door, he steps out taking my hand into his. He pulls me to him, my head hitting his chest.

I don't want him to go. This seems crazy, but you don't understand. What I'm feeling is something I never want to go away, and those feelings are here because of Kane. I'm not saying I love him. But I know I will. That's inevitable.

Kane kisses my forehead one last time. Closing my eyes, I try to memorize the feeling of his warm lips on mine.

He lets go and walks to his truck. His boots crunch under the gravel of my driveway and my head tilts to the side looking at his butt. He has a big butt for a man, and I'm appreciating that right now in his tight Wranglers.

He climbs in and starts his truck, "Lock your door," he yells out the window before pulling away. Nodding my head, I watch as he drives away.

Nothing can take the smile off my face.

One Week Later

"In here." I yell as I try to pull myself off the ground. I was mopping the kitchen floor, and I slipped. Every time I try to stand I slide back down to the ground. I spilled soap and was attempting to clean it up.

Kane walks around the corner and looks down at me on the ground. "What happened?"

"I slipped and fell. The floor's wet, and I can't stand." I huff out and try to push myself back off the ground again. My feet slide out from under me again. Landing onto my belly with a thump.

"Sit still Sydney. You're going to fucking hurt yourself." He growls and walks over to me.

His hands go under my arms and he lifts me up. Smiling, I wrap my arms around his neck. He kisses the corner of my lip and walks with me in his arms toward the living room.

He sets me down on the couch and stands in front of me with a small smile on his face. "How is my baby today?"

Grinning I stand up and kiss him. His hand trails up my waist to my hair. Licking the seam of his lips I deepen the kiss. Kane growls and fists my hair in his hands and pulls my head back so he can take control of the kiss.

His hands drop from my hair and go to my ass. I can feel each of his fingers as they squeeze my butt cheeks before lifting me off the ground. My legs go around his waist and I can feel each sway as he walks.

My back hits the wall, hard. Pulling back, I take a deep breath. His lips trail down my neck. He can take my virginity now. I feel like I'm being burned alive!

"Fuck me," I moan.

"Not yet, sweetheart." He chuckles against my neck.

"Kane, you're killing me," I ground out, frustrated.

"Why didn't you say so?" He raises up and gives me a wicked grin. He carries me upstairs and into my bedroom. I'm thrown onto my bed.

Gulping, I manage to get out an, "Oh shit," before I'm left speechless. The tongue on that man.

Later that week

Snuggling deep under Kane's neck I trail my hand up and down his belly. Thick arms pull me closer to him. He presses a kiss to the top of my head. "Kane. Why did you stay with your mom when she did what she did? You were a kid, but you could have gotten out."

He sighs and pulls me closer to him. "Because she was my mom. I loved her even though she was a shit mother. She wasn't always like that. I held on to the times where she was a great mom. A mom that baked me cookies, sang to me, and tucked me in at night."

"I couldn't leave her. I wanted to make sure she was safe. I put myself in front of her even as a kid so her drug dealers wouldn't hit her. I made sure she would eat. I did what I possibly could for her. It was a shit life. When she over dosed, I ran. I lived on the streets for years." He trails his fingers down my spine while I blink back tears at what my sweet Kane has been through.

"I was hard around the edges. My demons haunting the shit out of me. Still to this day I'm haunted. But I'm not going to let those demons haunt what I have." Sitting up, I look at him not caring I'm butt ass naked.

His eyes connect with mine, hard and serious. My body wracks with chills at his expression. "I'm not going to let those demons haunt what I have because, baby, I'll fight harder for you. Always."

I let out a gasp as my heart skips a beat at his words. That man… Jumping up I wrap my arms around his neck at a loss for words. One thing for sure is I'm falling hard for this man. He is perfect in every way.

seven

Two weeks later

Kane and I have been together for one month. We didn't discuss it. It just happened. To some people that doesn't sound very long, but we spend every waking moment together. Kane? It's hard to explain someone like him. Over the last month I have come to know him on so many levels. His demons, his sadness.

Kane has changed, but not in a bad way. He's protective, caring, tender and passionate. He's the kind of man who opens the door before you but smacks your ass as you walk in. He's controlling, and it drives me crazy, but I know he does it because he cares.

Since that first date, Kane has become my world. My

almost every thought is on him. He's the last thing I think of before I go to sleep and the first thing I think about when I wake. He stays the night a lot.

My phone ringing brings me out of my thoughts. Walking into the kitchen, I grab it and hit talk.

"Hello?"

"Hi. Want to go out tonight? I really want to go to a bar." Braelyn asks.

Braelyn has become the old Braelyn over the past month. She is still scared a lot, but every day I see more of the old Brae popping out, and I think a huge reason for this is Ethan. There is something there between them.

"Sure! Want me to pick you up?"

"That will be great. Be here at nine?"

"Sure, babe. See ya later." Hanging up, I go and collapse onto the couch reading my new favorite book.

Getting a text, I pick up my phone and wince. It's from Kane:

Kane: Want me to pick up some dinner?

Me: Girls night with Braelyn. Sorry.

Kane: No, have fun. Where are you going?

Me: Bar.

Kane: Be careful and call me if you drink so I can come and get you.

Me: I will. ☺

Picking my book up, I veg on the couch for the rest of the day.

I pull up at Ethan's house at ten until nine. I'm wearing a tight red dress that shows off my curves. It goes past my thigh so it's more than decent. It shows cleavage but not a lot.

Walking up Ethan's porch steps, I walk on inside. Hearing yelling, I run into the kitchen. Ethan is towering over Brae who has her arms crossed across her chest with an angry expression on her face. Looking between, them, I ask "What's going on?"

"You're not going out like that," Ethan growls at her.

"Yes I am!" she yells and stomps her foot.

Getting a good look at Brae, I understand why Ethan is having a meltdown her dress is really short; the back of it, well there isn't one. Her cleavage is having a race of who can pop out of her dress first. This isn't going to be good. Braelyn is wearing what they call 'a little black dress'.

Leaning back against the wall, I can't wipe the smile off my face. Braelyn isn't one who allowed anyone to tell her what to do, and Ethan is the kind of man who thinks his way is the right way.

"I repeat. Your ass is not going out in that." He steps closer to her so they're touching. Braelyn's eyes narrow, and I can image horns sprouting from her head.

"What did you just say?" she asks in an eerily calm voice.

"You heard me." He arches an eyebrow at him.

She steps around him and walks over to me. "Let's just

go." She grabs my arm and all but pulls me toward the door.

Then Braelyn is pulled away from me. She squeals as Ethan throws her over his shoulder and carries her up the steps. She bangs her small fists on his back. "I'm going to murder you, Ethan!" She screams loud enough to wake the dead.

I take a seat on the couch because I know Ethan won't stop until she changes. I get why Ethan doesn't want her dressed like that. She was raped. Every guy who sees her dressed like that won't be able to keep his hands to himself.

She walks past me with her arms crossed across her chest. She's wearing a longer black dress that shows less cleavage. Her jaw clenched tight she walks out onto the porch.

"Sydney. Call me if you need anything," he tells me but looks at Braelyn standing out on the porch. Nodding, I walk outside.

"You ready?" I ask Brae as we climb into my car.

"That fucker," she curses and slumps into her seat. Biting my lip, I try to control my laughter.

"How did he get you to change?" I ask curious.

"He changed me himself," she grounds out while staring out the window.

Nothing can stop my laughter this time. "Oh God, that's great."

She starts laughing a few moments after I do. "God, that man makes me want to commit murder."

"I understand that. Believe me," I mumble the last part.

"Let's have some fun tonight." Brae grins and claps her hands mischievously. Shaking my head, we ride the rest of the way to the bar in silence. Braelyn looks out of the window deep in thought. It's really a club, but I have the habit of calling it a bar because I'm a small town girl.

This club just opened a year ago. Purple, blue, and red strobe lights are everywhere even on the outside. It's not very busy yet, which is a good thing. I'm not much for crowds.

"We're here," I tell her as I park the car around the corner so we can actually leave when we want to. Drinking tonight will be very doubtful. Braelyn needed this night, and it's going to be about her.

Grabbing my wristlet and phone, I open my car door. Stepping out, I slam my door closed and walk over to Brae who is still sitting in the car. Not moving.

Opening her door, I peer inside. "What's the matter?"

She looks up at me, fear written on her face. "I'm scared," she barely whispers.

"I know, honey. I'm not drinking tonight. You have fun, and I won't leave your side. You've been through hell, Brae. You need to let loose and have fun. You need to live." Grabbing her hand, I pull her out of the car.

"Thank you, Sydney." She gives me a hug before letting go. A small smile on her face, she stands tall with her head held high. Smiling proudly, I lock my car.

It's almost completely dark out. Braelyn grabs my hand and looks around wildly at her surroundings. Squeezing her hand, I hurry to the front doors.

We are carded and then we go inside. Brae visibly relaxes. Looking around the room, I look for somewhere to sit. Spotting a table off to the corner of the room, I tap her shoulder then point in the direction of the table.

She nods and we walk to it. The loud music blares through the speakers. Braelyn sits in front of me across the table. Turning on my phone, I see five texts from Ethan and one from Kane.

Kane: you make it?

Me: Yes, just made it.

Ethan: You guys make it?

Is she okay?

Call me if you need anything.

Please watch over her Syd.

?

Shaking my head, I message back.

Me: I have my Taser, and I'm not drinking. She won't leave my sight. Everything will be okay, Ethan.

Another message pops onto my screen from Kane.

Kane: Be safe.

Me: I will I promise.

Ethan messages back, but I ignore it. Brae is chewing on her thumb nail nervously.

"Let's get you a drink." Standing up, I pull her from her seat and straight to the bar.

An hour passes and Brae has a nice buzz going. We're on the dance floor dancing, keeping our distance from everyone else. Making sure my purse is on me, I keep an eye on the crowd around me.

Running my hands up my body, I shake my butt seductively. Brae comes up to me and takes my hands so we're dancing together.

Three songs pass before she whispers into my ear, "I need to pee."

Laughing, I pull her in the direction of the bathroom. She stumbles behind in her four-inch heels. Moving through the crowd, we get bumped into a few times. One man runs into me hard. Hitting the floor, I land on my hip. That's going to leave one hell of a bruise. Glaring up at the man, I see him staring at something beside me.

My eyes widen when I take in Brae's expression. She is pale as a ghost. Her body shaking. The man is stepping closer to her with a creepy grin on his face. Climbing to my feet, I stand in front of Braelyn.

Braelyn presses her head into my back. My hands grip my dress. The man gives me a murderous look, but I keep backing up away from him. *Breathe, Sydney, stay calm. Braelyn needs you.*

"I'm not leaving here without her," the man roars in my face as he steps close enough that his stench has me gagging.

"Yes, you are." Not backing down, I slip my hand into my purse and pull my Taser out and put it behind my back. He's not looking at me but at Braelyn behind my back.

Shuddering, I keep backing up. His face contorts in anger with every step. This man's hair is so greasy and grime is covering his face; it smells like he's been washing his face in shit and pee.

I know what's going to happen before he does it. He rushes me, but my Taser is ready for him. I put the Taser to his neck and his whole entire body shakes before his eyes roll in the back of his head. He hits the ground with a thump—not moving.

Turning around, I grab Brae's hand we step over him and run to the bathroom. I may or may not have stepped on his balls in the process. Brae follows behind silently.

Stepping inside the bathroom, I lock the dead bolt on the door. Braelyn looks at me with tears filling her eyes. Shock is evident all over her face. Her face crumples as she collapses onto the ground.

Taking my phone out of my purse, I call Kane. He answers on the third ring. All my thoughts are focused on my Kane being here.

"Kane," I choke out.

"What happened?"

Rubbing my hand over my face, I don't take my eyes off Braelyn who is sobbing loudly.

"Braelyn's attacker is here. He tried to take her, but I got him in the neck with my Taser. We ran into the bathroom and locked the dead bolt," I answer quickly as I walk over to Braelyn.

"On my way. Stay there, baby. I'm going to call Ethan. I will be there soon, baby."

Kane

Sydney's call all but stops my heart. Imagining her in danger and not being able to do anything about it kills me. I didn't want her to fucking go. Fuck. Jumping off the couch, I run to the truck.

I spin gravel as I drive down my driveway. I call Ethan who picks up instantly.

"Kane, something has happened, hasn't it?" There's a hitch to his voice.

"Yeah, man, be waiting; I'm picking you up. The girls are fine." Hanging up, I concentrate on getting to Ethan and to my girl.

Ethan is standing at the end of his driveway pacing. He sees me and runs over, throwing the door open and jumping in.

"*Go!*" he roars at me.

Understanding his feeling, I floor it.

"Tell me what happened." His voice shows no emotion.

"Braelyn's attacker slash rapist tried to get her tonight."

"Fuck!" Ethan grounds out, punching my dashboard.

"Syd got him in the neck with her Taser and ran to the bathroom. Locked the door and is hiding out." I see him nod his head out of the corner of my eye.

Sydney. My brave woman. She put herself in danger doing that, but she did it to save her friend. If something had happened to her... My hand tightens on the steering wheel enough at the thought that I hear it crack.

My body stiffens as we pull up to the club. I know she is

close, and my body is begging to be close to her. Hold her in my arms to make sure she is okay.

Sydney

Sliding down the wall, I pull Brae into my arms. She sobs into my chest. Heart breaking sobs. I do the only thing I can: I hold her.

What the hell does that guy want? He's been following her for years. Did unspeakable things to her and then torments her for years. I was attacked by some random guy, but then… maybe it's not so random.

There was that letter on my car as I was leaving the mall. The guy is in jail so it could have been a prank or meant for someone else. I actually forgot about it until now.

"Sydney!"

Bracing myself against the wall, I push myself to my feet. Kane is here. Unlocking the dead bolt, Kane charges in and takes me into his arms. My body sags against him. Relief. He lifts me off the ground and my head goes to the crook of his neck. My arms around his neck.

"Baby, are you hurt?" He sets me down on the counter. My arms fall to my lap. His eyes search my body for injuries.

Touching his face with my hand, I reassure him. "I'm fine, Kane."

"Baby…" he trails off, his eyes full of torment. Shaking my head, I pull him to me again and rest my chin on his shoulder.

Ethan has Brae in his arms. A hand on the back of her head and the other hugging her tightly to him. Her body shakes from the sobs. Ethan's eyes are shut tight with his jaw set. He's mad.

My hands roam Kane's back and arms. Just being close to him makes me feel safe.

"Let's go home."

Nodding my head, I slide off the counter and down to my feet. Braelyn is holding onto Ethan for dear life.

"What if that man is still outside?" Brae asks against Ethan's neck.

"Baby, he's long gone. We know the owner, so we're checking the cameras. The man will be caught. He fucked up big when he decided to mess with my girl."

My eyes widen. Brae just got claimed. She has a smile tugging on her lips, but I'm the only one that can see it.

"Let's go." Ethan tells us and walks out of the bathroom with Brae in his arms.

Kane wraps an arm around me and pulls me into his side. We follow after Ethan. People don't notice us as we walk pass. People bump into Kane, but he is a man on a mission to get out of here.

Once outside I take a deep breath, finally feeling like I can actually *breathe*. Kane's truck is parked right by the door. Ethan's already in the backseat with Brae sitting in his lap. Kane pulls me toward the passenger door.

Opening the door, he picks me off the ground and up into my seat. He buckles me in and walks over to the driver's side. Slamming the door, he starts the truck and takes off, tires spinning.

The truck is silent except for the rumble of the engine. I watch as the lights of the town pass by in a blur. My mind is reeling from what happened. *I tased a man in the neck and squashed his balls. He wanted to kidnap Brae.* The shock of what's happened is wearing off.

A warm hand touches mine. Opening my hand, Kane laces our fingers together. Unbuckling my seat belt, I move over to the middle seat. My head resting on his shoulder, he kisses the top of my head. Closing my eyes, I try to keep the tears at bay. Brae's crying in the backseat breaks my heart. I can hear Ethan whispering to her. Kane squeezes my hand and lays our joined hands in his lap.

As soon as we get to my house, I walk straight upstairs. Kane sheds his shirt and hands it to me; I wear one of his shirts to bed every night. He climbs into bed and opens his arms for me. I lie on Kane's chest with his arms wrapped around me as he trails his fingers down my arm. Goosebumps break out across my skin and I snuggle deeper letting out a deep breath.

The house is quiet. Too quiet. My mind won't shut off from everything that happened. "Kane, tell me something about you."

His hand stills. "Baby, there isn't anything to know about me. My life growing up was hell and then I went to war."

Sighing, I say, "Yes, there is more to you, Kane. Growing up like that doesn't define you. It doesn't change the way I see you." Propping myself up on one elbow, I look him directly in the face. "We all have demons, Kane. Some are deeper than others. You can't let those demons dictate your life. You *are* someone. You are someone to *me*. You make me happier than I have ever been in my whole entire life. Since being with you, you put me above everything else. You want to protect and care for me."

Kane eyes never leave mine. His face is full of raw emotion. "Baby…" he starts, but I stop him with my mouth on his.

This kiss changes everything. This kiss is so much more than a kiss. I have fallen for him. Hard. I know he feels the same. You don't need the words to know someone loves you. You can tell by the way they look at you. When Kane holds me, it's like I'm his world, and I'm the only thing holding him together.

His hand sinks into my hair, and he lays me gently down onto the bed without breaking our lips. His body lying on top of mine, his other hand framing my face gently, he leans up so he is looking down at me. His eyes are full of emotion. Mine are showing him the same.

He lays his head at the crook of my neck. Wrapping my arms and legs around him, I let out a deep breath and close my eyes.

I drift off into a deep sleep. Kane's body never leaves mine the entire night.

Today is my mom's birthday. We're all getting together for dinner. Grabbing her gift off the counter, I hurry out the door and into my car. My mom is turning forty-five-years-old, but she doesn't look her age. Most people think we're sisters.

Smiling, I turn up the radio and sing along when "Yours" by Elle Henderson comes over the radio. It's been two weeks since the incident at the club. Braelyn is doing better, but she's closed into herself again.

Kane and I have become closer. That night changed everything. Everything is intensified. I love him. I've never been in love before and this happening is so fast it's overwhelming.

Pulling in front of my mother's house a few minutes

later, I see I'm the only one that's here. Chase is bringing the guys' Sergeant.

Walking into the house, I see my mother cooking; I offered to cook, but she wouldn't let me. Pulling her into a hug, I tell her, "Happy birthday!"

"Thanks, baby." She pats my back before turning back to the stove.

Laying her gift on the island, I ask, "Do you need me to do anything?"

"You bring the food to the table?" She motions to the food across the room.

"You should have let me cook, Mom." I huff as I pick up the first huge dish of food. She waves her spatula at me.

"Pish posh. Do as I say."

Setting the plates on the table, I go back to the kitchen to spend some time with Mom.

"How are you and Kane?" She gives me a sly smile.

Not able to keep the grin off my face, I say, "Everything is great."

She laughs under her breath. "I knew everything would turn out, honey. The way that man looks at you…"

"Mom, I love him," I answer honestly. She turns around to look at me.

"I know you do, honey. He loves you too." She grins.

The roar of a truck coming up the driveway has me running out of the house. I haven't seen Kane in two days. Too long in my opinion.

The screen door smacks against the siding as I go onto the porch. He steps out of his truck. His black t-shirt is tight around his broad shoulders, bulging at his arms, and loose around his waist. The tattoos on his arms are bright and glowing in the sun.

Running down the steps, I tackle him in a hug. My legs go around his waist, and his hands go to my butt to hold me up.

"Hi, sweetheart." His breath tickles my ear. Shuddering, I raise up to meet his gaze.

"Hi," I whisper back before sealing my lips to his. He growls low in his throat as he bites my bottom lip. Gasping, I press him harder to me while his hand flexes on my ass and pulls me closer, if that's even possible.

"Get a room!" someone yells from behind us.

Pulling back, I look behind Kane's shoulder. Chase is leaning against his truck laughing at us, an older man standing beside him. Smirking, I flip him the bird. Tapping Kane's arm, I motion for him to put me down on the ground.

Getting a good look at my brother and Kane's Military Sergeant. He's freaking hot for an older guy. He even has tattoos.

Kane sets me down but doesn't let go of me. Instead, he tucks me close to his side.

"Holy hell. I just came." A woman's voice says from behind me.

My eyes widen. Who the heck is that? My head shoots around like the exorcist.

A very pregnant woman and Brae are standing by a car. Brae looks down at the ground, blushing.

"I'm Jessica." She smiles and walks over to me.

Returning the smile, I shake her hand.

"I invited Jessica, if that's okay. She's new to town," Brae pipes in.

My mom pops her head out of the door. "Let's eat, everyone."

"Damn. There must be something in the water," I hear Jessica mutter under her breath, and Chase chuckles. Shaking my head, I make my way to the dining room. Kane pinches my butt hard. Jumping, I smack him equally as hard in the chest. He winks.

My mom puts more plates on the table. It's like freaking thanksgiving with the amount of food this woman made.

"Mom," I call her.

She looks up at me. I point over at Jessica. "This is Jessica." I then point at the Sergeant who is standing toward the back. "This is Ethan's and the guys' Sergeant."

I watch as she looks at him with a blush on her face. The Sergeant walks toward her. "Nice to meet you, I'm Dave." He extends her hand for her to shake.

Blushing deeper, she shakes his hand. "Nice to meet you too."

Looking at Ethan wondering if he's witnessing the same thing, I see that he's scowling at them both. Laughing silently, I pull out my seat to sit down.

My mom giggles and sits down too. My mom has never reacted this way toward a man. She never even dated to my knowledge.

We all sit down and eat together. Chase and Jessica

have us laughing so hard I'm crying. Jessica is like a more pervy Chase.

The Sergeant, who I now know as Dave, has had his undivided attention on my mom. I really hope that something comes out of this for her. She deserves to be happy. More than anyone else I know.

Kane has his hand on my leg. My body is noticing all too much at how close his hand is. Sucking in my bottom lip, I squirm in my seat. If only his hand would slide a little bit closer.

"Everyone want to go out on the back patio?" my mom interrupts my thoughts. Everyone gets up and follows her outside.

"I could watch that man's ass all day every day." Jessica grunts and tilts her head to the side to look at Chase's butt.

Laughing at Chase's stunned expression, my face runs into a hard back. Grabbing my stinging nose, I back up. "What the fuck?" Kane growls at Ethan.

"What are you doing?" I ask Mom, who is standing stoic on the porch blocking the door. Her face is pale and looks scared.

"Kane," I stutter out worried about my mom.

"Mom, what is it?" Ethan pushes her to the side so he can see what's wrong.

"No. No. No, no, no." She shakes her head in disbelief backing up. She swings around to look at me with wide eyes. Something is seriously wrong.

"I finally found you, bitch," a deep voice says from outside.

My mom gasps but only just shakes her head in disbelief. Everyone pushes their way outside. Kane holds me tightly to him. Seeing the man, my eyes widen. He looks a lot like Ethan. This man is evil; you can see it on his face and the way he's leering at my mom. Kane is stiff beside me. He moves so he is in front of me and the other half of my body is hidden by Chase so I'm only able to peek out slightly.

The man is staring at my mother evilly before his eyes glance over the rest of us. He can't see me. His gaze snaps back to my mother who has tears rolling down her face. *Who is this man? How does he know my mom?* Pushing away from Kane, I start to go to my mom.

"Where's our bitch of a daughter?" he roars at her.

My head shoots back like I've been smacked. Kane's body stiffens, and I can feel the rage radiating off of him. Putting my hand on his back, I peer around him once more.

This man has this vibe about him that just *screams* malice.

"Ah I see, Evelyn. You have a new dick to suck." He laughs darkly, and I can hear his foot creak on the steps.

Beside me, I see Chase grab Ethan who is about to charge the man.

"Who the fuck are you?" Ethan yells.

"Ethan, is that any way you're supposed to talk to your father? Speaking of children, where's that blonde bitch that took you guys away from me? She was the whole entire reason for your leaving." He makes a huge deal out of looking around the field and the driveway.

Kane's hand touches my back, pressing me harder into him. Fisting his shirt, I try to stay completely silent. I'm scared out of my mind, but I know Kane won't let anyone hurt me. I always dreamed my father was a good guy. Now my hope of ever having that is shattered.

"Get off my property now! I give you one fucking minute before I kill you myself. You will not touch a hair on my daughter's head. You kidnapped me." Her voice hitches at the end.

My heart stops. *My mom? Kidnapped? Oh my God!* I try to hold in the sob, but it slips through. Kane starts backing up toward the door.

"*You!*" he yells.

Kane stops backing up and lets his arms fall from my back.

"You, you big fucker. What's behind you?" Kane stiffens.

"None of your damn business, that's what. I advise you to get your ass off this property before I remove you myself." Kane's voice is chillingly calm.

"Ahh, you're hiding something. Is that my daughter?" He cackles, and I can hear him walking around.

"Here, bitchy bitchy bitchy. Come give your daddy a hug," he taunts me. My hand grips Kane's shirt tighter. Closing my eyes, I try to block everything out. I peek around Kane.

The man sees me and a grin comes across his face. "Well, well, well. It's my daughter, the slut," he gloats at me. "*You took everything from me!*" he screams, spit flying from his mouth.

He takes a step toward me. Kane pushes me back gently and then walks up to the man until they are nose to nose.

"I won't fucking tolerate you talking to my woman that way. I don't care who you are, where you're from. You better get off this property or suffer the consequences. Your choice." Kane is a couple of inches taller than him and twice his size. Any other person would have been intimidated.

Shuddering, I hug myself. "Just because I don't have her today, I *will* get her another day. Something happens to me? I have someone else who wants her just as bad. Wants to make her suffer." My father licks his lips before bringing up his hand. He makes a gun symbol and makes a pop with his mouth likes he's shooting me.

The man is too busy looking at me to notice Kane rearing his hand back. He punches him hard on the jaw, his head snapping back with his eyes rolling in the back of his head. He falls to the ground with a thump.

My eyes never leave the man who is lying on the ground. Unmoving. This man planned my attack. He all but admitted it. That letter I got wasn't an accident. It was because of him.

What kind of father would do this to their daughter? I slide down to the ground holding my head trying to wrap my head around this. All these years I thought something happened to my dad and she didn't want me to know. No, this man is crazy and *kidnapped* her.

The silence around me is deafening. Nobody moves; the

only thing you can hear is their breathing. Warm hands touch my arms. His smell envelopes me in a cocoon of security as he pulls my hand away from my face. Looking up, I see Kane staring at me with concern. Lifting my arms, I wrap them around his neck.

He lifts me off the ground and my legs wrap around his waist. He hugs me tightly to him. My face on his shoulder, tears running down my face and soaking his shirt.

I can feel him walking, but I don't look up. A second later I feel the couch cushions under my legs as he sits down. Snuggling deeper, I all but try to crawl into him. His hand is on the back of my head pressing me into him where I can hear his ragged breaths.

He kisses the top of my head, and I let out a sigh. Everything will be okay. I have Kane.

I must have fallen asleep. Looking up, I see my mother sitting beside me and Dave sitting beside her, holding her hand.

My mom notices I'm awake, so she scoots closer and frames my face with her hands.

"Baby, I'm so sorry."

"Mom, don't be sorry. I'm so sorry that you had to go through all of this," I start.

"Baby, that man. What he said to you…" A new batch of tears roll down her face.

"Mom, it's okay. Trust me, I'll be fine." Giving her a reassuring smile before turning to Kane, I tell him, "I need to go to the bathroom."

He nods, and I can feel his eyes on me as I walk out of the room.

After doing my business, I hurry back to Kane. He's sees me coming back and his body relaxes. This event has put him on edge. Standing in front of him, his hands go to my hips. He pulls me down into his lap, holding me close.

Ethan sits on the couch in front of us. He's looking down at the ground with his elbows resting on his knees.

"The police came and got him while you were sleeping," Kane whispers into my ear.

"I need to tell you guys everything. I tried to protect you, but this changes everything." She looks at me and then back to Ethan before she starts.

"Twenty-seven years ago, I was kidnapped." Ethan's jaw clenches and he looks over the wall by the door.

"I was walking home from work and this guy lured me into this house. I just moved to the city, and I was a country girl and where I grew up, I trusted everyone. He invited me in, and I thought why not?" She takes a deep breath and looks at her hands. "I was stuck in that house for four years. I never left, my parents think I'm dead. I was in Hell for years and I got pregnant with Ethan."

"He wasn't ever mean to Ethan; I was beyond grateful for that. This man thought that everything he was doing was normal. The only thing that kept me going was Ethan and my unborn child. Living in a basement apartment day in and day out was depressing." She wipes her tears from her face and looks straight at me.

"You were born, Sydney. He didn't like that you were a girl... actually, I'm not sure what it was. The way he looked at you was evil, pure hate. He wanted to kill you. I heard him plotting to kill you during one of the rare times he let me out of the basement. I was in the kitchen cooking his dinner, so I took Ethan and you, and I never once looked back. I hitched a ride with a trucker. Every few months I would pack up everything and leave again, because I was scared he'd find me and hurt my babies." She sniffles and looks down at the ground, ashamed. Then her face crumbles. My strong mother who has done everything she possibly could for us is sobbing heart breaking sobs.

Crawling out of Kane's lap, I sit down beside her. When I pull her to me, she wraps her arms around me, sobbing onto my neck. Feeling a tap on my shoulder, I see Dave staring at my mother. His hands are lifted as if he wants to pick her up. Nodding my head, I let my arms go, and he picks her up off the ground. She sobs into his chest as he carries her upstairs.

Ethan's whole entire body is red; he is about to explode. I lean across to the other couch, placing my hand on his knee. "Ethan, it's going to be okay."

His head snaps to me. "Okay? Are you fucking stupid? He has it out for you, Syd. He tortured Mom." He stands up and punches his fist through the drywall.

"Hey! Don't ever talk to her like that again.

Understand?" Kane tells Ethan.

"I'm sorry, Syd. Emotions are running high right now." Ethan shakes his head and paces the room.

Kane stands and stalks over to my brother. "You're not the only one. But, you have no right to talk to her that way. Not my woman. He and his buddies are a threat that I plan to eliminate."

Standing up, I put my hand on Kane's arm. "I'm fine, Kane. Ethan didn't mean anything."

"I felt helpless when you were scared, and that's a feeling I'm not used to nor one I will tolerate. You bring shit out of me that I haven't felt before. You're my everything, and I will protect you with every fiber of my being. I will dedicate myself to cherish, love, and protect you at all costs. Your happiness means everything to me."

Stunned, my mouth drops open. He takes my face into his hands and leans down to gently kiss my forehead. I'm left speechless.

"I approve," Ethan says from behind me.

Kane nods his head. "Doesn't matter if I had it or not. She's mine." Looking back and forth between Ethan and Kane, I'm confused. My brain is warped from Kane's admission. Did he just admit he loved me?

Hours later we finally head home. I'm absolutely exhausted.

"I hope my mom will be okay," I finally say, breaking the silence.

"If she is anything like you then she will be fine." He smiles and kisses my hand.

I'm headstrong, stubborn, and not someone who backs down easily. Today, I felt helpless. My dad being that way shocked me. He admitted that he planned my attack, the letter… I'm left reeling, not able to wrap my head around it.

As we pull up in front of my house, I notice that all my flowers have been cut and thrown to the ground. The swing is thrown out into the middle of the lawn.

"Sydney, I want you to stay in the truck," Kane tells me as he looks at my house.

He grabs a gun out of the middle console and steps out of the truck. Of course I'm going to follow him. There is no way in hell I'm staying in the truck by myself. As soon as Kane has his door shut, I open my door and hop out. That turns out very well considering I land right on my butt.

"I told you to stay in the truck," he growls as he helps me off the ground.

"You told me, but that doesn't mean I'm going to listen," I argue.

"Stay behind me, Sydney, I mean it."

"Okay! I will." I throw my hands up in defeat. He takes a hold of my hand and leads me into the house. Someone obviously trashed my yard, but hopefully nothing inside was damaged.

Walking up the porch steps, Kane walks straight for the

door. When he jiggles it and it's still locked I sigh with relief, but he shakes his head no at me.

"Could be the backdoor."

He takes my key out of my purse and unlocks the door. He pulls me through the house checking to make sure everything is clear. He lets go and walks into the kitchen.

Hearing a crash, I nervously whisper, "Kane?'

"Everything is okay," he reassures me. Letting out a deep breath, I walk in the kitchen. On the floor, a vase is shattered and white roses mingle within the glass. Kane is holding a card in his hand.

"What is that, Kane?"

He hands it to me. *Gotcha now, Bitch. See you soon. This time no one will stop me. I'm watching your every move. Your father was stupid and exposed himself, but not me. I'm always one step ahead of you.*

Letting the letter fall to the ground, I realize I have to tell Kane about the other letter.

Nervously, I turn to look at him.

"Kane? I... uhh... I have to tell you something."

"What is it?"

"This isn't the first time I have gotten a letter."

"What do you mean, Sydney?" he asks calmly, but I can see his struggle to remain in control.

"One month ago I found a letter on my car. I thought it was an accident or something. Now I know it wasn't.

"Sydney!" he growls and runs his hands through his hair angrily.

"I'm sorry! I was scared, and I was in denial, okay?"

"Sydney, promise me you won't hide things like this from me again. You're putting yourself in jeopardy. Don't you understand that I would do anything for you?" He runs an angry hand over his face.

Tackling him with a hug, I tell him, "I'm sorry. I don't know what I would do without you, Kane."

He rubs the back of my head and back. "You won't have to find out, sweetheart."

nine

We're staying at Kane's house instead of mine. Honestly, I don't want to be at my house knowing that I've been watched and someone that's out to harm me knows where I am. I've never been to Kane's house. We've always planned to stay at his house, but something always came up.

He lives close to Ethan where all the houses there are really nice. We pass by Ethan's house and keep on driving until he slows down by a driveway with a huge gate. He pulls up to a pole with a keypad and after opening his window, he enters the code.

The gate opens, and I get a good view of the house. It's an old country-style home. White with huge white pillars that reach to the third floor. Black shutters and huge windows show the glow of inside of the house. A chandelier hangs on the porch.

My mouth hits the ground. I knew Kane had money considering he owns several businesses, but this? I never expected this. I look to Kane, to his house, and back to Kane.

"Wow."

"Come on, sweetheart, let's get inside, and I'll cook you some dinner."

He gets out of the truck and walks to my side. He lifts me out of the truck, but my eyes never leave the house. This is my dream house.

Kane tugs on my hand, bringing me out of my thoughts. He leads me up to the front door, unlocking it, he disarms the alarm beside the door. He steps out in front of me, and I am hit with smell of new leather. The whole entire house is wood and the interior is southern, right down to the horse shoes like my mother's.

"Go change, sweetheart, I'm going to start supper. The bathroom is right through those doors."

Grabbing my bag off the floor, I walk to the bathroom. Sitting down on the toilet seat, I rub my temples, stressed out about everything. Sighing, I slip on one of Kane's shirt and a pair or panties. The shirt comes almost all the way to my knees.

Picking my bag up off the floor, I open the door and set the bag on the couch. I can smell something frying. Following the smell, I turn the corner to see Kane slaving over the stove. Definitely not the worst sight. Mmm, a woman could get used to this.

Walking over to Kane, I smack his butt, hard. He jumps in shock and turns around to look at me. Giving him a sly look, I knock the spoon off the table beside him. I mumble an exaggerated, "Oops!" before bending at the waist with my butt straight into the air.

A sharp pain on my back side has me yelping. "What was that for?" I flutter my eyelashes at him.

He smirks at me and turns the stove down on low. Gulping, I watch with wide eyes as he stalks toward me. I back up until my back hits the island in the middle of the floor.

"What was that, sweetheart?" he asks in a cocky tone.

Giving him an innocent look, I say, "Nothing. What are you talking about?"

"Hmm, baby, if you want to play just tell me. It's not good teasing a man who wants to fuck you." He leans forward so his mouth is next to my ear before whispering, "Hard."

"Oh shit," I mutter to myself as a finger trails my inner thigh.

My legs almost buckle. Kane arches an eyebrow at me before lifting me up onto the island as he steps between my legs and slams his mouth onto mine. A deep moan escapes me as his lips caress me gently. I bite his lip hard. The kiss turns wild, passionate. My breathing becomes erratic, feeling like being burned alive. My tongue licks his bottom lip.

His hand snakes under my shirt and up to my tit. Sucking in a sharp breath as the tip of his finger touches my nipple, I press myself harder into his hand needing *something*. Anything.

He takes his mouth from mine and kisses his way down to my neck. Tilting my head back to give him better access, my eyes close at the sensation of his hot lips kissing my neck with gentle nips.

"Raise your arms up, sweetheart."

Opening my eyes, I lift my arms above my head. He lifts the shirt and throws it across the room. He unsnaps my bra next and it hits the floor. The cold air makes goosebumps cover my chest and arms.

His heated gaze has me withering, waiting with need for his next move. His fingers hook around my panties. I start to lift my hips so he can pull them off, but he rips them from my body. My eyes widen. I'm completely bare to this man and it feels so much more than just being naked.

His hands rub my thighs and hips; his eyes connect with my hooded ones before he drops to his knees. *Oh my God, is he?* My question is answered when he grabs my hips and slams his mouth to my pussy.

All the air leaves my body once his warm tongue circles my clit. "Umm holy shit!" I yell out, as he pulls my clit into his mouth and sucks.

"Oh my God!" My hand slams against the island trying to grip something. Giving up, I lie down on my back.

Kane's hand grips my calf and throws it over his shoulders, pulling me impossibly closer to him. I intertwine my fingers through his hair, holding him to me. The strokes of his tongue goes from hard to soft, slow to fast.

He sucks my clit hard and sticks a finger in my pussy. *"Kane!"* I scream out his name as a powerful orgasm shoots through me. My whole entire body jerks at the power of it.

Kane lifts me up into his arms with my head lying on his chest. I lie still for a minute to control my breathing. It feels like my heart is trying to beat out of my chest.

"Kane?"

"Yes, baby?"

"Can we do this again sometime?" I ask him with a laugh.

"Anytime." I can hear the cockiness in his voice.

He steps back and looks at me. Blushing, I try to cover my body. He's seen me naked plenty of times, but this feels different.

His hands stop mine. "No, don't do that, baby. You're the most beautiful woman I have ever seen. Don't hide yourself and especially not from me. Your body is amazing and don't ever doubt that. If someone else thinks differently, fuck them. I'm the only person that's going to see your body, and I'm the only one that needs to. Listen to my words. You're. Mine. Yes, baby, we have been dating, but this is me claiming you from now until the future."

If it's humanly possible, I just fell further in love with him. Smiling at him, I try to control my emotions that want to come burrowing out. I don't doubt what I feel for this man. He came out of nowhere and took root in my heart, and I never want him to let go. A moment doesn't go by without me thinking of him.

"Sweetheart, go relax on the couch, and I'll bring your dinner." He places a kiss on my lips and sets me back on the ground.

He picks the tee off the ground and hands it to me. Smiling shyly, I take it from him and slip it over my head.

Taking my first step, I sway to the side slightly. My legs still aren't cooperating correctly and I can hear Kane laughing at me. I hobble like an old person into the living room. Spotting the couch, I all but collapse onto it. My eyes droop, and I close my eyes for a moment.

Something nudges my shoulder. Cracking one tired eye open, I see Kane on sitting on the coffee table in front of me. His face is red like he's trying to hold in his laughter.

"What are you laughing at?" I groan at him sleepily.

"Baby, I love walking into the living room seeing your ass up in the air," he says between laughs.

Looking back to see what he is talking about, I notice the t-shirt had ridden up in my sleep and my white butt is showing. My head is laying on the couch, but my bottom half is up in the air with my knees in my belly. My girly bits are out and waving to the world. Sitting up quickly, I blush, reaching to cover myself. *How did I fall asleep like that?*

"Here's your food, baby." He hands me a steaming plate of steak and potatoes. My mouth waters at the smell. Taking my fork, I dig in. Today has taken a lot out of me. So much so that when the juices of the steak hit my taste buds, I can't help but groan.

"Baby, groan like that again, and I won't be able to restrain myself."

Looking up, I see him staring at me darkly. Coughing, I give him an innocent smile before telling him, "Ummm, I'm sorry?"

"Shit, you're not sorry." He slightly chuckles and takes his plate from the coffee table. He sits down beside me and turns on the TV. Flipping through the channels, he settles on racing, which I absolutely hate.

Turning to face him, I give him my most pitiful look with my lip puckered out slightly.

He looks over at me for a second and looks away. I continue to look at him with puppy dog eyes. He looks over again and closes his eyes. "Sydney," he groans.

"Yes?" I ask innocently, making sure my dimple pops out.

"Fine!" He hands over the controller, and I turn it on to Steve Wilko. Best show ever. Nothing better than watching Steve throw chairs.

I give him a sweet kiss on the cheek. "Thank you, baby."

"At least it isn't some girly shit like Kim Fashion or something like that," he mutters to himself.

I can't stop the laughter from that one. "Kim who?"

"Kim Fashion or some shit," he tells me between bites and looks at me like I've lost it.

"That's the best one I have heard yet," I say between laughs.

"Baby, you've lost me." He's looking at me with an arched eyebrow.

Smacking his chest, I say, "It's Kim *Kardashian*."

"How was I supposed to know that?" he asks with a

chuckle.

After we finish our food, Kane and I cuddle up on the couch. He grabs the blanket from the back of the couch and tucks me in.

Craning my head back to look up at him, I say, "Kane?"

"Yes, baby?"

"I'm glad I'm here with you." He smiles at me sweetly.

"I'm glad you're here too, sweetheart. No other place I would want you to be. Let's go to bed."

Rolling off the couch, I stand and wait for Kane to show me the way. His house is huge and absolutely gorgeous. His arms slide under my legs as he sweeps me off my feet bridal style.

"What're you doing?"

"Carrying you."

"I know that," I tell him, rolling my eyes.

As we go up the huge steps, I get a good look upstairs. The entire second floor is nothing but rooms. *Wow, so many.* It's decorated really well. *Too well for a man to do it.*

"Who decorated your house?"

"Some chick I hired after I bought the house."

"Ahh, okay." *That makes sense.*

He carries me into the bedroom. There is a fireplace in front of the bed across the room. The bed is in the middle of the floor. He sets me on the bed, and I bounce slightly. He stares down at me before stripping off his shirt. My hands itch to touch his abs and the tattoos covering his chest.

"Raise your arms, baby."

I let out a deep breath and lift my hands above my head. He tugs on the bottom of my shirt and pulls it over my head. My hair tie gets caught in the shirt and hair flies down around my face. I'm completely naked. I keep my hands on the bed beside my hips, not daring to cover myself. Letting him know I trust him.

He lifts me back into his arms. Gripping his neck, I hold on. He climbs onto the bed and moves to the center of it. He lays me down gently, grabs the blanket lying at our feet, and covers me up. My head goes to his chest with one leg going over one of his.

Closing my eyes, I fall asleep to the sound of Kane's steady breathing.

Groaning wakes me up from my sleep and it's not the good kind. It's a moan full of pain. Sitting up quickly, I see that Kane is thrashing in his sleep, obviously having a nightmare. My brother has them, and I've been woken up many times from hearing him cry out in his sleep.

"Kane," I whisper and nudge his shoulder. I know better than to stay too close to him and back out of swinging distance. When he doesn't wake up, I shake him harder. His eyes snap open then he raises up and looks around quickly searching for an intruder.

When he finally looks at me I ask him, "Are you okay?"

He only nods his head with a blank look on his face.

Crawling toward him, I touch his arm. "I'm right here."

His eyes are haunted. This dream made him relive some horrific things. His arms reach for me, and I oblige by crawling into his lap and hugging him to me. He hugs me back tightly, his breathing erratic, trying to control his emotions.

"Do you want to talk about it?" I hold him tighter as he shakes his head no. I feel helpless, wanting more than anything to take his pain away. This is the first time he has ever done this in the many times we have spent the night together.

"You okay?" I ask him again.

"I'm okay, sweetheart, just a bad dream." He presses a kiss to my forehead.

He gently sets me off his lap and lays me back onto the bed. With me on my side and him behind me, he tucks me close to his body, his powerful arm around my midriff. Closing my eyes, I fall into a restless sleep.

One Week Later

As I slip on my shoes, I look into the mirror. My brown hair is in wavy curls, my eyes are lined with eyeliner and a couple coats of mascara. I smooth the white dress that hugs my hips and smile at my reflection. Kane is taking me to a fancy restaurant.

"Babe, you ready?" Kane calls from downstairs.

"Yeah, I'll be right down!" Grabbing my gloss off the counter, I stuff it in my bra. I am *not* taking a clutch just for lip-gloss. Seeing the stairs that could mean my impending death due to the heels on my feet, I feel like scooting on my ass like a kid so I don't break anything. Gripping the rail, I make my way down the stairs.

Kane is standing by the door. He looks up as I walk

down. His eyes widen and his mouth drops open. Blushing at his reaction, I duck my head.

Kane walks to the bottom of the steps and takes my hand as he tells me, "Sydney, you look absolutely gorgeous."

"Thank you." I blush and pretend to smooth my dress when what I'm really doing is drying my clammy hands from the nervous sweat accumulating on my palms.

"Turn around I want to see the back."

Grinning wickedly, I turn. The back is low cut and rests just above my butt. He trails a finger down my back as a shiver wracks my body.

"Yeah we are not fucking going anywhere."

Turning around I look at him in shock. "What?"

He pitches the bridge of his nose frustrated. "Baby, do you even see yourself? You're fucking hot. Every fucker who sees you will be staring at you with his tongue hanging out like a dog in heat. Do you want me to commit murder tonight? Nobody ogles my woman but me." His hands wander to my butt and squeeze hard.

"Why don't you just pee on me and get it over with?" I roll my eyes at him.

"My come on you isn't enough?" He gives me a smirk.

Well. Shit. He's got me there. "You have a point." I laugh at him. "Come on let's go, Kane. You know I'm one-hundred-percent yours. I don't want anyone else." Giving him my sweetest smile, his face softens. *That is how it's done, folks. I can hear the sound of a whip now.*

"Fine, but I'm not happy about it." He takes my hand

and we walk to the door together. "Do you have everything?"

"Yep." I whip my lip-gloss out of my bra to show him. His eyes widen for a second before he chuckles.

"You put shit in your bra?"

"Uh. Yeah? Why not? They are there for more than licking and nipple twisting." I grab ahold of my boobs and give them a jiggle.

"The shit you say, Syd, blows my mind." He laughs and opens the door.

"Yeah, yeah, yeah." I wave my hand around.

Walking out to the truck, I get a bad case of the ankle breakers. I look like a newborn horse. No heels for me tonight. Kane sweeps me off my feet and carries me the rest of the way.

"Those things are death traps."

Looking up at him, I say, "Tell me about it." After settling into the front seat, I smile at him.

"Uhh, Kane."

"Yeah?"

"Can you go grab my flats?" I tell him sweetly. He rolls his eyes and walks back into the house. *What did I say? Whipped.*

Pulling up in front of the restaurant twenty minutes later, Kane, always the gentleman, walks over and opens the door for me. Another car pulls up beside us. Kane takes my hand and helps me out of the truck. Smiling appreciatively, I situate my dress that rode up in the back slightly.

Walking hand in hand, we stride toward the restaurant. When he lets go of my hand and wraps an arm around me tightly, he holds me in a way that feels like he's shielding me from something. Looking at him confused, he doesn't acknowledge me. He's staring straight ahead. You would think nothing is wrong if it wasn't for the pissed off expression on his face.

"What is it?" I whisper to him. Nodding his head behind us, I peek over my shoulder. The man that pulled up behind us is walking close behind. He's staring at my butt without even blinking. He catches me looking, but he just keeps staring. The woman next to him is watching and she looks down sadly. Nobody deserves to be with someone like that.

"Umm, yeah that's creepy," I mutter.

We stop at the entrance so Kane can open the door and that's when I feel the man's breath on the back of my neck and his belly touching my butt slightly. Jumping forward, I try to get away.

"Back the fuck up, dude," Kane snarls at him and pushes him away. The man throws his hands up in defeat and backs farther away. Noticing the woman gone, I hope that she leaves this man's sorry ass.

"Kingston?" The waitress asks.

Kane nods.

"This way." She grabs two menus and leads us to our

table. Kane places his hand at the small of my back.

The restaurant has a brown stone fireplace with an illuminated flame flickering. Each table has a small candle sitting on top giving off a romantic glow with the lights dimmed.

The table she leads us to is a window seat, and she sets the menus down. The chair is high off the ground and the seat of the chair hits my waist. Putting my feet on the rail in front of the chair, I manage to pull myself up to my seat. My feet are dangling a good foot off the ground—I feel like a child.

Kane snickers. Not looking up from my menu, I warn, "Don't say a word."

"I wasn't saying anything."

Looking to the side of my menu, I glare at him.

"You're so fucking cute." He grins at me.

I put the menu in front of my face so I can hide my smile.

"Sydney?"

Putting the menu down I look at Kane. "Yes?"

"Why didn't you ever have sex before this? Don't get me wrong I'm so fucking glad that you haven't ever been with anyone else." He puts his hands on the table before him.

Clearing my throat, "I made a promise to myself a long time ago that my first time will be with someone who I care about, and I know this person is it for me." I pause to gauge his reaction. His eyes widen before a smile comes over his face that gives me butterflies.

"Most girls say they will wait for the special someone, but rarely does that happen. I really wanted to wait. I couldn't bear the thought of my first time being with someone I didn't care about. Not that there is anything wrong with having sex with whoever you want. This was my choice." I smile at Kane and tuck a piece of hair behind my ear.

"The moment I met you, I knew you would be that person. Don't ask me how I knew, but I just did."

Kane leans over the table and kisses me softly. A kiss that I feel all the way down to my soul. This kiss is filled with love. Something I've been dying to tell him. I love him. This man would protect me with his life, he loves me without restraint, he's my best friend. My everything and my forever. I never knew what I was missing in life into this man. He completes me.

"What are you doing, Kane?" I ask him as he stands up from his seat.

"Leaving?" He looks at me confused. *He's not leaving without paying the check, is he?*

"You didn't pay the check!" I hiss at him shocked.

"Baby, I own this restaurant," he says with a chuckle.

What? My mouth opens and closes like a fish out of water. *Why didn't I know this?* "Why didn't you tell me?" I finally get out.

"I didn't think it was necessary." He shrugs his shoulders.

"How many do you own?" I still can't wrap my head around this.

"A couple. I also own a few other places here and there. Isaac and I own a construction business. Chase and I own a place for kids to get away, learn self-defense, get a hot meal."

"Wow," I drag out. Sliding out of my seat, I walk over to Kane who immediately intertwines our fingers.

Kane opens the door and I walk out ahead of him. My eyes go to the man standing next to the street light. He's staring at us. Stiffening, I wait for the man's next move.

"What's the matter?" Kane asks when he notices my expression.

"Do you know that man?" I point in his direction.

"No, I don't," Kane says darkly and starts walking toward the man. The man notices and backs up before climbing into a truck a few feet away. Kane stops walking but stares down the man. Kane is the sweetest guy, but as soon as I'm in any sort of danger, he does a one-eighty ready to do anything to keep me safe.

The man starts his truck and rolls down the passenger side window. You can see only his hand and he acts like he's shooting me—just like my father. Gasping, I move farther away from the truck.

"Sweetheart, let's go." Kane turns around and has his arm around me. He keeps me walking slightly in front of him. The beeper for the truck goes off and he lifts me inside the truck. He opens the driver's side and steps in.

Once Kane buckles me in I lay my head against the window. *Why does this keep happening to me? What did I do to deserve this?* Being in danger and having to look around every corner for something to attack me is exhausting.

I am so lost in my thoughts I don't remember the ride home. Opening my door when we get to the house, I let Kane help me down. He doesn't let me go and my legs go around his waist, his hand flexing on my ass. Tonight I'm ready and I'm tired of waiting. I love Kane, and now is the time to tell him. I have no doubts, and I have no doubts about him loving me. You don't always need the words— just looking into someone's eye gives you all the reassurance you need.

Grabbing Kane's head between my two hands so he is looking at me, I say, "Kane, please, I'm ready. It doesn't matter the time or how. It's going to be perfect no matter what. As long as I'm with you. Because I love you, Kane, so much. I love you more each and every day."

His eyes search my face and then he kisses me softly, lovingly. Letting me know everything I need to know. Butterflies swarm my belly as he walks upstairs with me in his arms.

When he enters his bedroom, I notice the golden glow surrounding the room. Turning around, my mouth falls open on what's before me. Rose petals are on the floor and covering the white comforter. Candles surround the bed.

Turning to Kane with tears in my eyes, I manage to say, "I can't believe you did all this."

"You deserve it and more. I had a little help from Braelyn." He wipes the tears away.

Rubbing my thumb over his cheekbone, I seal my mouth to his. This kiss is something that can't be described. It's passionate, and I can *feel* love coming off Kane.

Lost in the kiss, I don't feel him moving until my back hits the soft bed. His lips make love to mine as his hands move over my body. He tugs at the bottom of my dress, and I lift my arms above my head so he can take it off.

He gently pushes me back onto the bed so he is hovering over me on his elbows. "You're beautiful, Sydney, on the inside and out. I can't believe that you're mine. I don't deserve you, but damn I'm selfish. You giving me this…" He trails off and I see tears mist in his eyes, but he blinks them away. Clearing his throat, he continues, "You giving me this. I don't have the words to describe how I feel. Just know this, Sydney, I love you so fucking much. You consume my heart and soul. I never thought I would fall in love. With my shitty past I don't deserve you. But you accept me, and I will do whatever it takes to love, protect, and cherish you for as long as you let me. You, Sydney, are everything to me, no doubt about that. What I feel for you is unwavering."

By the time he finishes, tears are pouring down my face. My strong, beautiful Kane just told me he loves me. For the first time in my life I know this is where I'm meant to be. I never knew something was missing until I met this man.

"Kane," I sob out.

He brings his lips to me in a slow, sweet kiss. He pours everything into that kiss, and I know he means every single word he said.

His mouth trails down to my throat, so I crane my neck to the side to give him better access. His mouth kisses the top of my breasts. Lifting my back slightly, I unsnap my bra and throw it across the room.

His mouth descends to my nipple. He swirls the tip with his tongue before sucking deep. Groaning, I scratch his back. He turns to the other one and gives it as much attention until I'm withering with need.

He kisses his way down my body, and I feel his breath on my pussy. Shuddering, I lean my hips up for him to take, but he lifts my leg and kisses the inside of my thigh. He kisses all around but never touches my pussy. This teasing is torture.

Right when I start to grab his head and jerk him to me, he licks me from top the bottom. I almost shoot off the bed. Crying out, I grab his head. Looking down at Kane, I see him looking at me with hooded eyes. It's erotic seeing him biting, licking, and sucking. My body is in overload. He sticks one finger inside me, and then the other, leisurely moving them in and out of me.

"Oh my God, Kane." Throwing my head back in ecstasy, I grip the cover. My legs stiffen and trap his head between my legs as the orgasm powers through me.

Lying with my arm thrown above my head, I try to catch my breath. I feel the bed dip as Kane climbs off.

A minute later Kane's body covers mine. Opening my

eyes, I see Kane shirtless, and after looking farther down, I see that he's completely naked. He leans down and kisses my mouth slowly.

"Are you sure you're ready?" His eyes search mine for any hesitation.

I nod my head. "I haven't been this sure of anything in my life."

He takes the condom off the nightstand and raises up to slip it on. I stop him because I don't want anything between us. "I'm on the pill, and I know you're clean. I saw the papers where you just got checked last week."

He looks at me shocked before a slow smile comes over his face. He throws the condom over his head. A giggle escapes at his antics. He leans down and kisses me again, his hands stroking my body lovingly before they slip between my legs. He rubs my clit again until I'm soaked. I can feel the head of his dick pressing against my opening.

Bracing myself, I think, *this is it*. Kane looks down at me with so much love. His eyes never leave mine. He cups my head with his hand and whispers, "I love you, sweetheart," before he presses the head inside of me. It's not painful, but it's definitely not comfortable. He braces himself and lets me adjust.

I grit my teeth. "Just do it." He pushes himself in all the way to the hilt. Crying out at the searing pain, I turn my head to the side and bite my lip. Tears form in my eyes and fall down my face.

"I'm so sorry, baby." His kisses my forehead.

The pain starts to recede a few minutes later. I can feel

his hand between us again. He rubs my clit and the pleasure starts to overtake the pain. Feeling a delicious fullness, I tip my hips to test the waters. *Not bad.* I grip Kane's butt and grind him into me.

"You can move now," I assure him.

"Are you sure?" he asks, concerned.

Smiling at him, I place my hands on his shoulders. He pulls out and slowly back in. Our eyes never leaving one another as we make love. This is exactly how I pictured my first time. Each touch, each caress—filled with love.

The pressure at the bottom of my belly is slow but steady. We come together, and the look on Kane's face is one I'll never forget. One of raw pleasure.

I roll onto my belly exhausted. Kane runs his hand up and down my back. Grabbing the hand touching my back, I pull it over my so I'm hugging it. His front touches my back as I kiss the palm of his hand.

"This is the best night of my life, Kane," I whisper out into the candle-lit room.

"Mine too, baby." He kisses the top of my head before he crawls off the side of the bed.

"Where are you going?"

"I'm running you a hot bath." His firm butt walks into the bathroom. Stretching my muscles, I sit up and look down to see there's blood on the blanket. Which is white. *Great.* Standing up, I pull the blanket off the bed and set it on the chair across the room. I'll wash it in the morning.

Walking into the bathroom, I see Kane is testing the water. Leaning my hip against the door frame, I just watch him. He notices me watching and gives me a big smile. That smile makes me swoon. I love him so much.

"Come here, sweetheart."

Walking over to him, he stands up. He is towering over me and my head barely hits the bottom of his chest. He wraps his arms around me and holds me close for a second. Sighing against his chest, I wrap my arms around him.

"Get in." He lets go of me and gently pushes me toward the tub.

"No, no. You go with me." I tug on his hand.

He scoops me off my feet and steps into the tub. Sitting between his legs, he massages my shoulders and back.

"If you keep doing that I will be asleep in seconds." I roll my neck as he massages my shoulders.

"We can't have that, can we?"

I hear a click and look back to see that Kane has a washcloth and a bottle of my body wash. He lifts my arm and gently washes it. Then he washes my body slowly.

Taking the washcloth from him, I then wash him. From his neck to his feet. If it's even possible, I feel that we're more connected now than ever before. It doesn't matter how long you know the person. It can be a week or six months—you know when you know.

He lifts me out of the tub again and dries off his body then mine. Walking to the bed, I collapse on top of it. Spent.

"Why is the comforter over there?" Kane asks from the bathroom.

"I. Uhh. You know virginity... losing it... things

happen." Feeling incredibly awkward and embarrassed, I cover my face with my hands.

"Ohh. I'll go get another blanket."

I lie on the bed spread eagle, but I don't give a flip. I'm throbbing down there. Whoever says that shit doesn't hurt is a big fat liar. The bed bounces as Kane climbs in. Rolling over so my head is on his chest, he covers me with the blanket, and I'm out.

The sound of creaking stairs wakes me. Cracking my eyes open, I see Kane walk into the bedroom. He's only wearing boxers and looks absolutely delicious. Twisting on the bed so I'm lying on my belly with my head propped up on my hand, I say, "Morning, sexy."

"Good morning, beautiful." He gives me a sly smile before kissing my forehead.

Slipping out of the covers the cold air hits my breasts and my hands automatically go to hide them. Kane's eyes darken as he looks over my body. I look down at my feet, blushing.

"Don't get all shy on me now, sweetheart."

That makes me blush even harder. *Dang it.*

Ring, ring, ring.

Walking to the table beside the bed, I pick up my phone. "Hello?"

"Sydney! We are having a girls' day. Manis', pedis',

massages, facials. We will be at Kane's in an hour to pick you up," Jessica yells into the phone and hangs up before I can argue.

Sighing, I put down my phone. Turning to look at Kane, I tell him, "Looks like I'm having a girls' day." What I really want is to spend the day with Kane.

"When will they be here?"

"In an hour," I grunt and walk to the shower. As expected, I'm really sore. Plus, Kane isn't a small guy. Turning the water on, I wait a minute to let it warm up. Stepping in, I pick up the shampoo just as the shower door opens and Kane steps in naked.

Gulping, I stare at his body. His body is hard as a rock and sculpted with abs that are begging to be licked. I'm one lucky bitch. He takes the shampoo from me while I'm staring at him like an idiot. It's like he knows what I'm thinking because he gives me his signature smirk.

He opens the shampoo lid and pours some into his hand. "Turn around, love." Doing as I'm told, I turn around. I feel his hands on my hair and then he starts rubbing the shampoo into my hair. The only person that has washed my hair besides me is my mom. The sensation is amazing—there's something calming about someone else scrubbing your scalp.

"Rinse," he orders. Going under the water spray, I lean my head back slightly because the heat feels amazing.

Kane's hands start to wander to my waist, my sides, my belly. My eyes shoot open and look down. Kane is on his knees before me.

"Lean against the wall."

Turning around, I lean against the wall away from the water spray. He then lifts one leg up and lays it across his shoulder. His hands are on my butt lifting me up higher until my other leg is off the ground.

His voice is gruff when he says, "Place your other leg on my shoulder."

"Umm. How can that work?"

He smirks at me, and I wearily do as I'm told. Lifting my leg up, I place it over his shoulder. He grips my butt hard and lowers his mouth down to my pussy. He sucks my clit into his mouth hard. Licking, sucking, nipping. He never touches lower than that because he knows I'm sore.

"Kane," I moan.

He takes my clit in his mouth again and sucks. Then his head moves side to side while sucking. Black spots cloud my vision.

"*Oh my God!*" I scream and hold his head tighter to me. He does this over and over again. Then it hits me like a tidal wave. I almost fall to the floor as I tilt to the side trying to grip something. Kane unhooks my legs from his shoulders and keeps me off the ground with my legs wrapped around him.

While he holds me with one arm he pumps some conditioner into his hand and massages it into my hair.

Are you okay?" he asks with a laugh.

"Never been better." I rub his back while laying my head on his shoulder.

"I need to put you down so I can wash you."

Nodding my head, he sets me down and washes me. Once every inch of my body is clean, he turns off the water and steps out first to hand me a towel before wrapping one around his waist.

He should be on my next book cover. Nah, I wouldn't want women ogling him. I'm selfish that way.

Walking back into the bedroom, I see my bag of clothes laying on top of the bed. He must have brought them upstairs. Glancing at the clock I realize I have just thirty minutes. Grimacing, I slip on a pair of shorts and tank quickly and run to the bathroom to finish getting ready.

Just as I'm finished getting ready the doorbell rings. There goes breakfast. I hear the door open and then squealing. I'm betting that's Jessica because I bet Kane hasn't put on a shirt yet.

Walking down the stairs, I see Jessica openly ogling Kane who is shifting side to side. Braelyn is rolling her eyes at her.

When the stairs creak Jessica's and Brae's eyes shoot to me. A huge grin comes over Jessica's face. *Yeah, she knows.* Ignoring her, I go straight to Kane.

"Bye, baby," I murmur against his lips.

"Bye." I back away and start to walk past when he pinches my butt. Jumping, I glare back at him.

"Okay, love birds, you will be back with each other

soon. We have an appointment to keep." Jessica claps her hands and then points toward the door.

I walk straight for the car not giving them a second to corner me until Kane is out of earshot. Slamming my door, I hear theirs slam next, and then…

"Oh. My. God. It happened." Jessica jumps up down in her seat which can't be an easy feat considering she is six months pregnant.

Blushing furiously, I look out of the window.

"Finally?" Brae asks next.

Biting my lip to contain my smile. I nod.

"She lost her virginity!" Brae squeals again.

"Yes, I did." I smile.

"How was it? Did you come?" Jessica asks too excitedly.

Looking back her, I give her a wicked smile. "Yes, I did; twice last night and again before you guys arrived."

"Oh my flippin' goodness! I'm so jealous." She crosses her arms and looks out the window pouting. Looking at Brae she has a huge smile on her face staring out in space.

"What's that look, Brae?"

"She went on a date last night!" Jessica pipes in.

I look at Brae curiously. "Who was it?" She smiles nervously.

"It was Ethan," Jessica pipes in again smugly.

I gasp, "What?"

She blushes but keeps quiet.

"About freaking time!" I push her shoulder slightly.

"Calm your tits, bitch. There might not be another

date," she tells me quietly.

"Yeah, right, and cows don't eat grass. Puhleasee," Jessica says.

"Which salon are we going to? I'm not getting a Brazilian wax! Hell no." I shake my head.

"Oh my God! I just now remembered!" Brae can't hold it in any longer.

Brae chuckles knowing the reason why because she was a witness.

I bang my head against the window knowing she is going to blurt it out.

"She glued her ass cheeks together with wax. She wasn't supposed to close her legs." Tears stream down her face with her laughter.

"Oh shit! You too?" Jessica yells from the backseat.

I look back at her, shocked. Her eyes widen like she can't believe she told us. We both laugh hysterically.

"Oh shit that's great." I wipe the tears from my eyes. "Plus my ta-ta hurts." I shift uncomfortably.

"Wasn't he easy, Sydney?" Brae asks angrily.

"Yes, he was. He was freaking huge. Hurt like a bitch, but the orgasm made up for it." I smirk at her and she rolls her eyes at me.

"I need a hot sexy man! My hormones make me horny all the freaking time. What am I going to do when I can't reach back there? I'm screwed," she cries out.

Me and Brae share a secret look. "Chase," we mouth at each other and giggle slightly. Chase is a total man whore, but I can tell him and Jessica have a little something going on.

Turning around I pat her leg. "Oh, honey, I will buy you the biggest vibrator." She sniffs and wipes her eyes and gives me a big smile. Disaster averted.

A few minutes later we pull up in front of the salon. Opening the car door, I walk to the back seat to help Jessica, who takes my hand to pull herself out of the car. We are greeted by a woman who leads us to a room to change into our robes.

A few minutes later, we are led to another room with three beds for our massages. Looking down at Jessica's belly, I think, *Yep, that's not going to work.* She sighs from beside me and knows it too.

"I'm pregnant; I can't lay down on my belly like that."

"We have a pregnancy table, it's no problem." The masseuse pats her shoulder and walks out of the room.

Brae and I sit down on the table just as a man comes in carrying another table that has a hole right in the middle. Jessica gives him an appreciative smile, while Brae and I gawk at him. He is one sexy man. He then struts right to me. "I'm your masseuse for the day."

I blush and look down at my feet. *Holy shit. Holy mother frigging shit. Kane is going to have a bitch fit, but hey, I don't get to choose my masseuse, right?* Two more hot men walk in and that makes me feel better.

"Please take off your robes and place this towel around your waist." The men walk out of the room to give us some privacy. Sliding onto the bed, I tuck the towel tightly around my waist. Brae starts giggling beside me and Jessica looks like she is in hot guy heaven.

"You're going to take off your shirt too, right?" Jessica asks the men as soon as they walk into the door. Brae and I look over at her, shocked.

The masseuse beside her chuckles and shakes his head no, then he gets busy doing what massage people do. I stick my head through the little hole and try to relax.

"Kane is going to die, Sydney." Brae's voice is muffled by the cushion.

"I know it." I giggle nervously.

"You have a protective man?" the one massaging me asks.

"Heck yeah. He's built like a Mack truck. Wouldn't want to cross him," she says with a laugh.

"That's okay. I'm gay."

"Ahh, okay, then that does help things for you, but let's take a picture and send to him," Jessica tells us both. I raise my head up to yell at her.

Brae raises up and forgets she doesn't have a top on as she sits up. Her tits are on full display.

"Brae, your top!" I yell at her. She looks down and her hands automatically come up to cover herself. She blushes all the way down to her toes.

After all the primping, I'm beyond tired. I walk into Kane's to the aroma of steak. Groaning, I walk into the kitchen to see him in his boxers slaving over the stove again. I forgot to eat lunch too.

"Hey, sweetheart," he says without turning around.

Walking over to him, I wrap my arms around him and rest my head against his back. I feel at home as soon as I get around him.

"How was your day?"

"It was great," I tell him. *Too cheery. You're giving yourself away.*

"How was the massage?" My eyes widen. *What do I say?*

"It was fine," I say, but it sounds more like a question.

"I really didn't like that man rubbing up on my woman." *Oh shit.* I move back so I can look at him.

"Your new pregnant friend sent Ethan a pic and then he sent it to me." He's still cooking the food. *Is he mad?*

"You're not mad, are you?" I ask nervously.

"I'm not mad, baby. I just didn't like him rubbing on you like that." He turns around and hugs me to him.

"He was gay," I blurt out and Kane chuckles.

He turns around and jerks my hips against his. "I don't care if he was a woman, a nun, or the freaking pope. I don't like anyone touching you." He smacks my butt and turns back around to finish cooking. Walking upstairs, I change into one of Kane's shirt. At least he wasn't mad.

The rest of the night is us just spending quality time with each other. We eat dinner, cuddle on the couch, and when we're finished, he carries me upstairs and falls asleep on my belly. Smiling to myself, I think about how lucky I am to have someone like him. Together, we have an unbreakable bond.

eleven

Ring, ring, ring. I roll over groaning. "Turn it off."

"I don't recognize this number; I better answer."

The bed shifts as he sits up in bed.

"Hello?" he says in his sexy morning voice. "It is," he tells the person on the phone.

Sitting up, I get the feeling something is wrong.

"What?" he asks, shocked. He stays quiet for a second listening. "I didn't know I had any family left."

My eyes widen, and I place my hand on his back. *Did a family member of his die?*

"Yes, I'm still here. Hang on a second." He takes the phone away from his ear and hits speaker.

"Continue," he tells whoever is on the phone.

"You're the only living relative left. Her daughter has no one. She was your mom's sister's daughter. Arabella is your cousin. Would you be willing to take her in? It's either you, or I will be forced to put her in foster care. She's had a rough go at life. Her mother was hooked on drugs really bad; she died of overdose. The little girl was found in a closet," the woman's voice tells us sadly.

Tears rush to my eyes.

"How old is she?" I ask not being able to help myself.

"She is three years old."

I look at Kane with my eyes full of tears.

"I'll take her," he tells the woman on the phone.

"No, *we'll* take her." I grab his hand tightly. Kane talks on the phone going over details and whatever else before hanging up so we can get up and get dressed. She will be here later this evening. She just lived two hours away. Grabbing my purse, we haul ass to Kane's truck. We have nothing for a little girl.

"We need snacks, clothes, toys, blankets, furniture and necessities. Oh shit. I don't even know!" I ground out, stressed.

Kane takes my hand and kisses the top of it. "We will figure it out."

Sighing, I lean over and kiss him on the cheek.

Kane picks up his phone and calls Ethan. He explains everything. We will need help getting the furniture up in time.

A few minutes later we pull up in front of a furniture store. Kane comes over to my side to let me out and we walk hand in hand up to the front doors. I can't believe this is actually happening. This poor little baby, she just lost her mother. I can only imagine the kind of hell she has seen or been through.

Kane smacking my butt brings me out of my thoughts. Rolling my eyes, I walk inside the front door that he holds open for me. Looking around the store, I realize I have no clue where to start.

Looking up to the sign that tells you where the kids section is, I head in that direction. As soon as we get to the back section I see a white bed that is fit for a little girl. It's a four-post bed with white curtains hanging from the top of the frame, and that wrap around the posts of the bed. It looks like a princess bed. Looking around, I see all the furniture that matches—the toy box, small dresser, and chest. The drawer knobs are adorned with jewels.

Grinning at Kane, I tell him, "This is it." He chuckles and goes to find a worker.

This is the day that everything changes. This little girl is going to change our lives forever. I never thought this would happen, but everything happens for a reason.

Later that day

"She is almost here, Kane," I tell him breathlessly. The social worker called and told us she was ten minutes out.

"I know, sweetheart." He looks down at me softly and holds me tightly in his arms.

Laying my head against his chest, I suck in a deep breath enjoying just being in his presence.

"You don't have to be here for this, Sydney." His arms

tighten around me waiting for my response.

"I know, Kane," I mutter against his chest before looking up at him. "I want nothing more than to be here for this little girl. Not one second did I doubt this."

His face softens before he brings his mouth to mine. Sighing, I pull him harder against me. He moves his lips tenderly over mine. When he pulls back, his breathing is labored. His lips go to my forehead, and he whispers, "I love you, Sydney."

Closing my eyes, I try to hold back the emotions I'm feeling. "I love you, too."

The sound of a car driving up the driveway has me looking out of the window. My heart stops. "She's here," I whisper to Kane.

He smiles and takes my hand. Together, we walk out hand and hand. Through the window of the car I can see a little blonde head looking all around her frantically trying to take everything in.

The social works gets out and walks to the backdoor. "How are you guys today?" the social worker asks as she opens the back door to the vehicle. She leans in and unbuckles the little girl.

Little feet hit the pavement as she climbs out of the car. My eyes shoot down to the ratty shoes that cover her feet. The worker pulls her into view and my heart breaks instantly. Walking down the steps, I'm itching to get close to her. To comfort her. Kane follows closely behind.

"Meet Arabella," the social worker says, and I let go of Kane's hand. Taking the last couple steps so I'm a foot away from her. She barely peeks at me before going back to tugging at the ends of her clothes.

"Hey, sweetheart." I bend down so I'm eye level with her. Reaching up, I touch her shoulder. She jerks back like I hit her. She looks up at me and her face crumbles as she starts crying. She's scared. Not knowing what to do, I take her into my arms. Her little face rests on my shoulder, her tears soaking my shirt.

Standing up, I place my hand on the back of her head and the other under her butt to hold her up. Warmth hits my back as Kane wraps his arms around us both. The social worker is staring at us with tears in her eyes.

Kane places his hand on her back and she jerks again from the contact. Kane drops his hand and he looks out at the field with his jaw clenched. He's pissed, and so am I. *What kind of mom lets her child get hit? What kind of fucking mother doesn't care for her child?* Today is the day this little girl won't ever have to worry about anything like that again.

"I have some papers here for you to sign. I checked everything, and it's obvious that you can financially care for the child. I checked your records and everything came back clean. I will be back in a week to check on things." She nods her head at Kane and points to go inside the house.

Kane puts his hand on the small of my back and leads me up the steps. Arabella is still wrapped around me tightly. Her little fists clenching my shirt.

"This way," he tells the social worker and points toward

the kitchen.

Her mouth is open as she stares around at the house. She turns to Kane. "Wow, your house is amazing." She then turns her head to the boxes of toys and bed things for Arabella. Her face softens and turns to look at me. Smiling, I hug Arabella tighter to me.

"I see you guys are well prepared." She doesn't say anything else as she follows Kane into the kitchen.

What do I do? Follow after them? Stay here? Deciding to stand at the door frame that leads into the kitchen so I'm in view but not close enough to think I'm eavesdropping, I watch as Kane signs some things and the social worker puts them into a file. "I will be on my way. It was nice to meet you." The social worker turns to Kane and then to me.

"You too," I tell her. Kane just nods but doesn't take his eyes off me. The door shuts a minute later.

What do I do now? Maybe she is hungry.

"Are you hungry, baby?" I ask her softly. I can feel her nod slightly against my shoulder. "What would you like?" I ask again.

"Pizza?"

Looking up at Kane I smile at him. Kane takes out his phone to place the order.

"Kane, I'm going to sit in the living room while we wait for the pizza."

He nods his head. His eyes are sad when he looks at Arabella. She reminds him of himself when he was a kid. The product of having to live with a mother who did drugs and did nothing to care for her child.

Sitting down on the couch, Arabella doesn't move. After a few minutes she starts to move around a little, and then she turns her head and her eyes connect with him. Her icy blue eyes have me sucking in a sharp breath. Her eyes are identical to Kane's.

I can feel Kane walk by us and sit down beside me. His hand touches my thigh as he looks down at the little girl. She sits up a little farther to get a better view. Looking at Kane, I notice him smiling at her slightly.

"Hey, baby," Kane whispers to her. He smooths her hair away from her face. She doesn't flinch.

She sits up all the way, her eyes never leaving Kane. Kane rubs his thumb over her cheek. Her eyes widen. Bracing myself, I prepare for her to start crying. To my utter disbelief, she lifts her arms and reaches for Kane.

She wraps herself around him like a monkey. Her little fists clench his shirt. Her face goes to his chest. Kane wraps his arms around her protectively. He gives me a pained look. I know how he's feeling. It's tearing me up inside at the thought of what made this little girl this way.

The doorbells rings and Arabella cries out and burrows deeper into Kane's chest. He holds her tighter. Putting my hand over my mouth, I try to hold in my sob. Kane leans to the side slightly and pulls out his wallet. He nods to the door. Nodding, I go to pay the pizza man.

Hurrying, I pay and grab the pizza, gently closing the door behind me not wanting to startle Arabella. Going to the kitchen I grab plates, two waters, and a cup of milk. Setting everything on top of the pizza box, I carry it back to the living room.

Arabella is still cuddling to his chest. "Food's ready."

Kane lifts her up so she sitting in his lap. Opening the box, I place a piece on each of our plates. Noticing that Arabella's eyes never leave the food, I quickly cut the pizza up into little pieces so she can pick it up and eat it herself.

Sitting down, I put the plate into her lap. She stares down at it for a second before she nervously looks around her like she's waiting for someone to snatch the food away any second. She slowly picks up a piece and lifts her to her mouth and takes her first bite. She barely bites into it before she starts chewing and shoves the rest into her mouth. Kane and I don't eat—we can't take our eyes off of this little girl.

Grabbing the sippy cup off of the coffee table, I hand it to her. She takes it from me and takes a dainty sip. Her eyes widen and looks down at the cup wondering what's in it. *She doesn't even know what milk is!*

Clearing my throat, I try to control my emotions. More than anything I just want to curl into a ball and sob. I want to take the pain away from this child. Make her feel safe and have her forget everything that happened to her.

She finishes the food and climbs off Kane's lap.

"Pee," she says quietly.

Shocked that she said something, I stand up slowly. Offering my hand for her to take, she wearily looks at it before slipping her hand into mine. Leading her to the bathroom she goes straight to the toilet and does her business.

"Let's wash our hands." Pulling out a little stool I lift her onto it.

Putting some soap in her palm, I turn on the water and help her scrub her hands. Bending down, I blow bubbles from her hands. She giggles. It's barely noticeable, but it's something. Smiling proudly, I rinse her hands and dry them with a towel.

"Want to show her to her room?" Kane asks from behind us. Turning around, I lift her down from the stool. She stares at Kane and then back at me.

Taking her hand, I lead her to the steps. She looks up at them before putting her foot on the first one. Kane walks ahead of us. We spent the last few hours putting everything up. Don't ask me how we did it, but we did.

Kane pushes her door open and walks inside, flipping on the lights as he goes. Turning the corner, she sees her room. Her eyes light up and her mouth opens slightly. She lets go of my hand and walks toward a doll laying on her bed.

She stops before she can touch it. She looks at me nervously. "It's yours, baby." She grabs the doll and hugs it to her. Backing out of the door, I pull Kane with me. We move out of the sight of the door. I wrap my arms around him and hug him tightly to me as I let go of the emotions that have been threatening to break free from the moment I met this little girl. His hand shakes as he rubs my back, trying to comfort me.

I can hear her inside of the bedroom playing with her toys.

"Kane," I start, but he shushes me.

"I know." He kisses my forehead before pulling me tighter against him.

"I love you," I say against his chest.

"I love you, too, baby. So much." He kisses the top of my head.

Closing my eyes, I take in the comfort of Kane's arms. Pulling back, I peek around the corner at Arabella. She's sitting on the floor brushing the doll's hair.

"I need to give her a bath," I tell him.

"Give her a bath, and I'll fix her bed for the night.

"Okay."

Walking back into her bedroom, I tell her, "Okay, sweetheart, it's time for a bath. Let's pick out your pajamas." I go to her little white dresser and pick out two princess gowns and hold them up for her to pick one. "You choose the one you want to wear."

Her little eyes light up again and she points to the purple gown.

"Good choice." I give her a wink and head to the bathtub. Pulling back the curtains, I run her bath. I can feel her watching me.

Turning around, I tell her, "Come here, sweetheart."

She slowly walks toward me, and I take her little hand. "I promise you that everything will be okay. Okay?" Smiling at her, she stares at me confused. Pulling her dirty clothes off her, dirt hits the floor as the shirt hits the ground.

A brown and yellow bruise streaks across her belly up to her ribs. It happened a while ago. Anger sweeps through me. Composing myself, I lift her into the tub. Pulling some bath paint out of the cabinet, I help her paint the tub—she draws little swirls.

After getting her bathed, she grabs her doll and we walk downstairs. She lets go of my hand and heads straight for Kane. She lifts her arms up, and he instantly picks her up. He sits on the couch with her, and I move to cuddle up to his other side.

"Look at her belly," I whisper into his ear.

"Can I see your tummy, angel?" He smiles at her. She nods her little head and moves so he can pull up the gown.

His eyes are instantly full of anger. The kind of anger that's ready to detonate. I feel the same way. I want to hurt the person who did this ten times worse. What could a child have done to deserve something like this? Nothing. No child ever deserves this no matter what they do.

Tucking my head against Kane's shoulder, he wraps his arms around us both. It doesn't take long before she falls asleep. Sitting up, Kane gets up and carries her to bed. Following behind him, I watch from the doorway as he lifts the child bar and tucks the blanket around her.

Walking into our bedroom, I take off my clothes as I go. His hand goes to my hips, turning me around. He gently lays me down onto the bed. Our eyes show the same emotion: we need this. He covers his body with mine as he slowly makes love to me, our eyes never leaving each other.

Screaming wakes me up from a deep sleep. Shooting up in bed, I look around frantically. Throwing the blanket back, I rush off the bed, but Kane is ahead of me. Following behind him, we run into Arabella's bedroom and find she isn't there. Another piercing scream comes from the closet. With three long strides, he's at the closet and all but rips the door from its hinges.

Arabella is curled up into a little ball on the floor. Her eyes are closed tight and little droplets of tears trickle down her cheeks. Kane lifts her into his arms, startling her, but once she realizes he has her, she rests her head on his shoulder.

Kane cradles her to his chest as she wraps her little arms around his neck. "Shhh, baby girl. I got you. No one is ever going to bother you again. I will make sure of that. You're safe here." He sways side to side.

He walks into our bedroom with her curled into his chest. Gently, he lays down on the bed with her. Crawling up beside him, I wrap my arms around her too.

"Fank you."

I look up at Kane shocked. This is the third time she has talked today. It's a small feat, but it gives us something. *Hope.*

"Nothing to thank, love bug." I kiss the top of her head and lie down.

Kane lies still with her on his chest.

LeAnn Ashers

I wake up to something poking my nose. Cracking my tired eyes open, I see wild blonde hair and large blue eyes staring at me.

"Hey, baby girl," I whisper softly. Kane is still asleep.

"Hi," she says sheepishly.

Smiling at her, I ask in a hushed voice, "You hungry?" Her little head nods up and down. Sitting up, I slide off the bed. Standing next to it, I raise my hands to see if she wants me to carry her. She lifts her arms. I pick her up and settle her on my hip as she lays her head on my shoulder sleepily.

Kissing the top of her head, we head downstairs. I gather all the ingredients for pancakes while she sits at the breakfast bar. I give her a spoon so she can help me stir. I always loved to help my mother in the kitchen.

"Want to stir, sweetheart?"

She looks at me confused. Taking her little hand, I place the spoon in her fingers. Moving her hand, I show her how. Her nose scrunches as she concentrates on stirring.

Thirty minutes later she is fed and Kane's breakfast is in the oven keeping warm. He must have been really tired because he is always up before me. Scratch that, he's coming down the stairs now—shirtless.

Clamping my legs together, I try to stop the ache. I crave him like my next breath. Butterflies swarm my belly as he comes straight for me. Standing up on my tiptoes, I wrap my arms around his neck. He picks me up off the ground and gives me a deep kiss that has my toes curling.

"Good morning, baby." He gives me another kiss on the

146

forehead and goes over to Arabella. He gives her a kiss of the top of the head. She smiles a little and it's absolutely beautiful. "Good morning, baby girl."

"Kane, go sit down, and I'll bring your breakfast." He gives me that crooked grin and sits down beside Arabella.

Taking his food to him, I go to Arabella. "You want to go play with your toys?" Her eyes light up, and I lead her upstairs to her bedroom.

"l will be right downstairs. I will be back soon to check on you." She goes straight for the dolls laying by her bed.

Walking back downstairs, Kane is sitting at the table still eating. Sitting down beside him, I ask, "What do we do now, Kane?" *I have no clue.* Of course I have been around little kids, but I know nothing about her. She has seen so much in her short life.

"I have no clue, sweetheart." He sighs and leans back in his seat.

So the rest of the day we just spend time together. Getting to know her and letting her get to know us. She is slowly coming out of her shell little by little. She's still very skittish and watches our every move.

"Arabella, want to see the horses?" She looks up at Kane with so much excitement and even lifts her arms up so he can pick her up. He grabs his shoes and then hands me hers. I slip hers on her feet before he opens the door and heads to the barn.

"Sydney, let's take her on a ride," he yells over his shoulder, and I grab my shoes excitedly. I love horseback riding. I practically run to the barn. Kane is standing by a beautiful bay horse that Arabella is petting on its nose as she stares at it in amazement.

"Take her, and I'll go grab your horse."

Giving him a nod, I turn to Arabella who is now staring at me. "How do you like the horse, sweetheart?"

"Wuv it!" she says, smiling. Kissing her head, I squeeze her to me. Horse hooves hit the concrete and this horse is a Palomino.

Kane takes Arabella from me and sets her on his horse. I go to the Palomino and hop on. Kane gets on the horse behind Arabella who's grinning from ear to ear.

"You ready to go, baby girl?"

We ride for hours before we let the horses take a break. Arabella and I walk off into the field. She looks sad and looks off in the distance.

"What's the matter, sweetheart?" I bend down beside her.

"I miss momma." She hangs her head down.

"Oh I know, baby. Your momma is in heaven. She's always with you in here." I touch her heart before pushing her hair behind her ear.

"She wants me to be sad. She huwt me." Tears roll down her face.

Taking her in my arms, I tell her, "I'm so sorry, baby. I promise to never ever hurt you." Leaning up, I wipe away all her tears. Her bottom lip trembles.

Taking her hand, I lead her back to Kane. This is the beginning for us. This curve ball changes our lives forever. I'm glad that Arabella came into our lives, and I know Kane feels the same way.

twelve

Two months later

Two months have passed since we got Arabella. We have had our ups and downs. I fall more in love with Kane every single day watching him be a father to that little girl.

Arabella is the sweetest little girl. She isn't afraid of us anymore. The scars of what happened to her before she got here will always be there and that kills me. Every single day I try to replace those bad memories with good ones.

"You ready to go, darlin'?"

Turning around, I see Kane leaning against the door frame. Giving him a shy smile, I nod. I still get nervous around him like we just went on our first date. He comes and grabs the cooler which is full of food to take it outside to his truck. I go to the living room. Arabella is sitting on the floor combing her doll's hair.

"You ready to go, sweetheart?"

She looks up and gives me a smile before standing up. Walking over to me she takes my hand. Leading her to the door, I put her shoes on.

"We meeting your momma?"

Looking up at her she is staring at me nervously.

"Yes, my momma." I tweak her nose which causes her to giggle.

"Will you be *my* momma?" Arabella places her little hand on my cheek.

The oxygen is sucked out of me. Blinking rapidly, I try to keep the tears at bay.

"I want nothing more, lady bug."

"Otay, Momma," she whispers and lays her head on my shoulder.

I love this girl as much as a mother can love her child. *No, she is my child. My baby*. She changed everything when she came into my life.

She pulls back to look at me before asking, "What 'bout Kaney?"

"Go ask him about that, sweetheart." Kissing her forehead, she starts squirming in my arms wanting down. As soon as her feet touch the ground she takes off outside to Kane.

Kane

Turning around I see *my* baby girl standing beside me. She

takes my hand and pulls me down so I'm eye level with her. She shuffles her feet nervously.

"What's the matter, baby girl?" I tip her chin so she is looking directly at me.

"Will you be my daddy?"

My heart stops. I want nothing more than to be her father. To be the person who will protect her from the world, to love her fiercely and unconditionally. To do anything for her. I want to be the man to walk her down the aisle when she gets married. If that ever happens—no one will be good enough for my baby girl. The person that she comes to when she's sad, the person who holds her hand when she's afraid to take that next step in life. The person she looks up to. This little girl came into my life and flipped it's on its head just like Sydney.

"There is nothing more in this world that I would rather be." I pull her to me and give her a kiss on the forehead.

"Wuv you, Daddy."

Emotions overcome me. Coughing to get the knot out of my throat, I say, "I love you too, baby girl."

Hearing sniffling from beside us, I look over to see Syd crying. Her tears break me every fucking time.

"Come here, sweetheart."

She walks over and cuddles up to my other side. *My girls. My world.*

Sydney

I watch as Kane holds Arabella to him. His eyes close and

his arms flexed around her protectively. She is so small compared to him. I start to cry at the overflowing emotion I feel. Kane looks up and motions for me to join them. Cuddling up to his other side, Kane hugs us both tightly to us.

"Okay, we have to go." I pull back.

Standing up, I take Arabella's hand to help her up. Kane leans down to give me a quick kiss. Even that little kiss leaves me breathless. He picks Arabella up and takes her to the truck to buckle her in her car seat.

He gets in and takes my hand. Smiling, I look at the window as we drive past fields of horses. The whole gang is there at the park waiting to meet Arabella. She has had a really rough time starting out with us and we didn't want to overwhelm her right away, so we kept her away from everyone. I think she's ready. It's been two months.

Pulling up at the park, I look back at Arabella who's staring out the window. I really hope she will be okay. My family is waiting at a picnic table. Letting out a deep breath, I unbuckle my seat belt.

"She'll be fine," Kane says then gives me a quick kiss on the forehead. Opening his door, he walks over to mine, lifts me down, and then opens Arabella's door. She smiles shyly at Kane as he unbuckles her and lifts her out of the truck. He puts her down and takes my hand and hers in his other hand.

Turning around, I see my family is waiting anxiously for us. My mom has her hand over her mouth. Dave has his arm around her. Ethan, Brae, Chase, and Jessica don't take their eyes off her. Arabella has Kane's eyes and hair color. Looking at Arabella, I see that she has stiffened up with her thumb in her mouth. She's scared. She sticks her thumb into her mouth as a nervous habit.

"She's scared," I tell Kane. He nods and picks her up off the ground. She hides her head in his neck. He closes his eyes with a clenched jaw. We both hate that she's so scared of everything. She's not scared of Kane or me anymore, but things around her frighten her. Something loud on the TV has her hiding in her closet. She hides food under her bed. I noticed this when I smelled something rotting.

Kane and I continue walking to our family. Nobody says a word. He kisses Arabella's head before whispering something to her. I can see her nod slightly. Then she looks up at everyone.

My mother sucks in a sharp breath. Arabella sticks her thumb back into her mouth, her eyes shooting to everyone sitting in front of her. Holding my breath, I wait to see what happens next. Once she looks at my mother she stops and then she looks at me.

"Dat your momma?" She points at my mom.

"Yes, baby, she is." I smile at her.

She lifts her hand and barely waves her hand at everyone then ducks her head, embarrassed. She's too stinking cute.

"Let's eat, everyone," my mom announces and Kane gets up to get the cooler out of the truck. I try to help Mom put food out, but it's not an easy task with Arabella hiding her head against my chest.

Bending down, I whisper into her ear, "Baby, these people love you and have been waiting to meet you for a long time. Especially my mom. They're not going to hurt you." I kiss her temple and raise back up.

Kane sets the food down beside us and begins lifting out the dishes I made. Noticing Kane is back, Arabella sits up so she is sitting up in my lap.

Kane has a way of making her feel safe no matter what. When she is scared, she gravitates to him. Arabella is used to people not being nice to her and thinks it's going to happen all the time. Her little body shakes. It breaks my heart. I want nothing more than to take away her pain. One day she will be unafraid.

Kane grabs a plate and fills it up for Arabella who is now openly looking at everyone. Shifting her, I move so I can place her plate in her lap.

Turning to Kane, I ask, "Can you grab her cup?" He nods and hands it to me.

Arabella's already eating her food. She used to shove everything she possibly could into her mouth too fast and she would get sick. It kills me knowing that this little girl went hungry. I can't imagine what she has been through, what she's seen, or had to endure. The image of the bruise across her belly has me gritting my teeth angrily.

Looking up, I catch Ethan kissing the top of Braelyn's head. My eyes widen, and I look between the both of them.

"When did this happen?" I voice my thoughts.

Braelyn blushes and turns to Ethan shyly before answering, "It just happened. I couldn't fight it." She shrugs her shoulders and smiles.

"That's a beautiful story, you guys." Jessica fakes sniffles and drastically wipes under her eyes.

Rolling my eyes, I look at Jessica who is now grinning evilly. Chase chuckles and winks at her. She immediately quits smiling. Uh oh.

"Oh hush, Jessica. Don't get me started on the fire down yonda!" Braelyn screeches at Jessica. Sucking in my lips, I try to control my laughter.

"If you say one more word, Braelyn, I will tell all your secrets. Including the specific dream." She grins wickedly and winks at Ethan.

Ethan gives Braelyn a saucy grin. "Do tell, Braelyn."

Her eyes widen and she looks like she is about to bolt.

"That's enough." My mom gives them her motherly glare. "Let's eat." Everyone grabs a plate and chows down.

After everyone eats, my mom turns to Arabella. "Would you like to go play?" She points at the playground.

Arabella sticks her thumb into her mouth. She looks up at me. Smiling, I nod my head, encouraging her. She pushes off my lap and slowly walks to my mom.

My mom takes her hand and leads her over to the playground. Nervously, I watch her reaction, ready to run to her at any second.

Hearing sobbing, I see Jessica lying on her side on the blanket crying. Her pregnancy hormones are all over the place.

Moving over to her, I place my hand on her shoulder.

"What's the matter, Jessica?" I rub her shoulder

soothingly.

"Seeing you with your child… it's beautiful. I'm also sexually frustrated." She covers her face with her hands. Brae rubs her head.

Looking over my shoulder to see Chase running over.

Nudging Brae, I nod toward Chase. She smiles and ducks her head to hide it.

Chase gets on his knees in front of her and pulls her up to a sitting position. He takes her hand away from her face and holds it in his hand. "Are you okay, love?"

She nods quickly.

"Then why are you crying?" He wipes away her tears.

"She's horny," Brae blurts out. My eyes go wide at Brae who is smirking at Jessica.

"Thank you for that, Braelyn. I was about to tell him that myself. Yes, I'm sexually frustrated." She blushes deeply. *She can blush?*

I look back at Chase, and he's grinning. Biting my lip, I try to contain my smile. "Honey, I'm sure your man is at home dying for you to come to take care of that."

Jessica's face whitens and her hands are visibly shaking. Taking her hand in mine, I ask, "What's the matter?"

She shakes her head frantically and looks down at her lap before looking back at Chase. "I don't have a husband or a man. I left my boyfriend as soon as I found out I was pregnant."

Brae sucks in a sharp breath, and I stiffen knowing what will be said next won't make anyone very happy.

"My boyfriend beat the ever-loving shit out me. A slap

here and slap there. I wanted to leave, but I was scared. Then the beatings got worse. I read a text and he's mixed up in some shady things. When I learned I was pregnant, I left and never looked back. I have moved from town to town every couple months or so. This baby is all I have. I was going to leave him before. The baby gave me the strength to leave." She sniffs and wipes away the stray tears.

"Sweetheart," Chase drawls out before taking her into her arms and pulling her into his lap. He is furious. His face and body movements show everything. Her body shakes as she tries to control her emotions.

What kind of person hits a woman? Hurts a child? There is some fucked up people in this world. I will make sure my child will know how to defend herself. To never ever let a man lay hands on her or treat her poorly.

I want Arabella to fall in love with a man like Kane. Who is protective, caring, tender, and loves unconditionally. Kane would lay down his life for me. I love that man with every part of my being. No woman should have less than something like that. Kane is my soul-mate. I thought soul-mates where an illusion made up in fairy tales until him.

Looking at the playground, I see my mom holding Arabella behind her protectively. Dave stands in front of them both. Dave was staring at a truck parked in the parking lot. You can see the man inside and he has a gang symbol like my father and the guy that attacked me. The air rushes out of my lungs.

"No. No. No. No." I mutter to myself. Turning to Kane, I smack his arm and point to Dave. He takes in the scene then jumps to his feet and runs over to them with me on his heels. Kane picks Arabella off the ground.

"Kane, I think we should go." I whisper to him anxiously.

He nods his head and wraps his arm around me protectively. Shuddering I peek over at the truck that's pulling out of the parking lot. I know in my gut that he was watching me. Kane leads us to the truck.

Kane helps me up and then buckles Arabella in. Leaning my head against the glass I try to relax. Kane slamming his truck door closed startles me. The leather seat creaks as he scoots over to me and takes me into his arms.

"It will be okay, sweetheart." He presses his lips to my temple and takes my hand in his. He starts up the truck and we head for home.

Cameron

Get to the fucking bar now.

Throwing my phone in the floor board I peel out of the parking lot. I got caught watching her. Grinning in satisfaction. Good, she needs to be scared. That bitch got away from me years ago. Not anymore, she is MINE. She was mine before she met that big fucker.

The first time I saw her I knew she would have been mine. She was walking to class on the college campus. I'll kill him for touching her, then I'll beat the fuck out of her for being with another man.

The fucker was supposed to kidnap her and bring her to me. I didn't expect for her to fight like that or that big fucker showing up. Taking my nails, I scrape them up my arm. I smile at the pain. Sydney is going to feel so much fucking pain. I got a bitch at home that will just have to do until I make her mine.

Slamming the door as I stalk into the fucking bar, pissed that I'm disturbed of watching Sydney. Spotting my dad, I walk up to him, "What the fuck is it, old man?" I ground out between my teeth.

"I need you to meet someone," he tells me and nods toward the man standing next to him who has a gang symbol on his face like the rest of us. He's based in another city. Arching my eyebrow, I turn around ready to go, I need to get back to Sydney. Not being close to her makes my skin crawl and my hands shake like a fucking meth head.

Walking towards the door, what he says next has me stopping in my tracks. "This is her dad. I just bailed him out of jail. You want that girl. Here is your help." He says in a sing song voice.

"What?" I growl and turn around to glare at my father.

"He hates her fucking guts," my father tells me with a smirk. Grinning, I turn to her father.

"She took my wife from me. She needs to fucking pay," he roars in my face. Spit flies from his mouth.

"Once I have her. She will." I can't keep the grin off my face.

"Let's get to planning then." He grins sinisterly.

Sydney

Once we make it home, I take Arabella upstairs to change into some play clothes.

"Mommy?" Stopping, I turn around to look at her as I'm getting her clothes out of the closet.

"Yes, honey?" I walk over and bend down in front of her.

"Who was dat man?" she asks with her blue eyes full of fear.

"He was no one, honey." I kiss her nose and slip her shirt over her head. Leaving her to play, I go join Kane in the bedroom. Spotting him sitting on the corner of the bed, I collapse on top of it, emotionally drained.

"Kane, I can't stand the thought of putting you guys in danger." My voice is muffled from lying face down on top of the bed.

"I love you, sweetheart. No more worrying about this. Let me worry about these things. This is my burden, not yours. Now go change." He pulls me off the bed and smacks my ass as he pushes me in the direction of the closet.

Closing the closet door behind me, I quickly change into one of Kane's long shirts and a pair of shorts. Walking back into the bedroom I see that Arabella has gotten my makeup and is putting it on Kane. Putting my hand over my mouth, I attempt to hold in my laugh.

Stepping forward, I hit my toe on the edge of the door frame, giving myself away. Kane turns around and his eyes are completely black with eyeshadow. I can't hold it in anymore—I bend over laughing at him. He gives me a smirk and lets her finish putting makeup on him.

After he manages to get all the makeup off, we cuddle into bed watching TV. Arabella is lying on her belly in front of us watching *Frozen*.

"What kind of fucking show is this?"

Looking over at him shocked, I smack his chest. "Language!"

"She isn't going to repeat shit. Right, Arabella?" He looks over at her.

She looks over at him innocently. "I'm not going to repeat shit."

I giggle at him as he looks at her in astonishment. He grabs her feet and tickles them. "Otay, I give up." She wipes tears away from laughing and goes back to her movie.

Kane grins from ear to ear. Taking his face in my hands, I pull him to me and give him a quick kiss. He grabs my hand and pulls me over his lap, my head hanging off the bed.

"What are you...?" I manage to get out before he starts tickling my sides and the back of my knees. Weird place to be ticklish I know, but I am. Thrashing my arms and legs, I try to get away.

"Get off of Mommy, Daddy."

All thirty pounds of my little girl lands on my legs as she

tries to tackle Kane, I'm assuming, but doing more damage to me. He falls over like she's injured him.

"Okay, I give up. You're too strong for me." He holds the back of his hand to his forehead.

"That's wight. You best be on good beehive, mister." Wagging her little finger at him with a scrunched up nose. She is so stinking cute.

"Yes, ma'am." He has his hands up in the air with a scared expression on his face. After she's satisfied that he's being good she crawls into my lap. "Mommy, can you read me a story?"

"Sure, baby girl."

Grabbing my phone, I click the Kindle app.

"What do you want to read?"

"I want a story how you and daddy met."

She cuddles against my chest and looks up at me with big blue eyes. Kane is staring at me with a small smile tugging at his lips.

"Once upon a time, a girl was shopping in the village when a bad man started to follow her. She was so scared. When she called her brother to come rescue her, he sent his best knight."

"Daddy!" she pipes in.

"Yes, your daddy. He came out and saved her from those bad men. That's the day that she knew your daddy would be a special part of her life. He saved the girl, and then they fell in love. Then we got the best present in the whole wide world."

"What?" Excitement shows in her eyes.

"You, baby." I tuck a stray hair behind her ear.

She points a finger to her chest. "Me?"

"Yes, you. You're the best thing that ever happened to us."

"She's right," Kane chimes in. Her head snaps over to look at him in. "You and Mommy mean everything to me," Kane tells her again.

"Weally?" Her bottom lip starts to tremble.

"Yes, love bug."

"I wuv you duys." She quickly hugs me and then jumps into Kane's arms. He closes his eyes and holds her close. He opens them a second later.

I mouth to him, "I love you." He nods and mouths back he loves me in return.

Arabella stays in Kane's lap for the next hour. She falls asleep, and he carries her to bed. He walks back into the room and locks the door behind him. *Oh, shit. When he locks the door you know that shit is about to go down.*

His clothes come off with each step he takes.

"Take your clothes off. Now," he growls. I jump off the bed in a hurry. Kane jumps on the bed and lies on his back.

"Climb on the bed and place your knees on either side of my face."

I give him a shocked look. "What?"

He gives me a sexy grin. "Do as you're told, sweetheart."

"You do know that I'm not good with orders, correct?"

"Get your ass up here, now!" he orders

"Jeez, okay, bossy much?" I strip off my clothes and

lean on the front of the bed. Getting down on my knees, I lift one leg over so I'm completely bare and open to him.

"Now what?" I ask breathlessly. I can feel his warm breath on me.

"Ride my face." He grabs my hips and slams my hips down on his face. His tongue instantly pierces my pussy. Throwing my head back, I moan. Instinctively, I move back and forth. His tongue flattens and strokes my clit.

"Holy shit!" I moan, and then I move again.

He takes my hips and moves them. He doesn't need to show me twice. I start to move. I move my hips over his face and he takes everything I have. His moves his tongue with my movements. I bite my hand trying to control my scream as the powerful orgasm overtakes me.

My body goes limp as I fall over to the side of the bed with my body quivering with aftershocks. His tongue is magic.

"Wow, that was fucking hot," I say breathlessly.

He flips me over so he is hovering over me and gives me that cocky smirk that is well-deserved. They should give him an award with a tongue like that. Leaning forward, I give him a deep kiss. His tongue swipes my lips. Groaning I take his lip in my mouth and bite down hard. He groans and wraps my legs around his waist, ready for round two.

His lips leave mine and trail down my neck. I can feel his breath on my chest and nipples. That makes them even harder, and before I can look down, he bites my nipple hard. Not to the point of pain, but the bite makes my back arch off the bed.

"Hang on, sweetheart. I'm going to fuck you. Hard. Place your hands on the headboard.

Hold on tight."

Before I can reply, he slams into me. He stops for a second to let me adjust. Then he hammers into me. We have fucked before, but this is raw. Throwing my head back, I try to keep my scream at bay.

"Oh my God. Harder." He does as he is told. He pumps into me impossibly harder.

"I'm coming," I cry out. My body lifts completely off the bed. Kane pumps a few more times before he cries out his release.

He collapses on the bed on top of me. Our breathing labored. Kane lifts his head up and gives me a slow, sweet kiss.

We slip some clothes on and he unlocks the door. Lying flat on my back, Kane lays his head on my boobs. My hands run through his hair. He sighs and cuddles closer.

"Sydney?"

"Hmm?"

"I love you."

"I love you, too, baby, so much." Lifting my legs up I wrap them around him so I can hug him tighter to me.

thirteen

Something pokes my nose and wakes me up. Opening my eyes, I see blonde hair flying in the air as she lays back down pretending to be asleep. Kane's hand moves at my side letting me know he is awake. Closing my eyes, I pretend to be still sleeping. She touches my nose again. Opening one eye, I see she lies back down with her eyes covered. She thinks if her eyes are covered then her whole body is hidden. She giggles. This time I don't close my eyes, but I move my head directly above hers. She moves her hands and sees that I caught her, squeals, and then slides off the bed.

Laughing, I collapse back onto the bed. Kane threads his fingers into my hair to give me a good morning kiss.

"Morning, baby," he says again my lips.

"Morning." I kiss his cheek before throwing the cover

off me to track Arabella down.

"Wait," Kane tells me and grabs my arm again.

Turning around, I look at him. A small smile tugs at his lips. "You're beautiful, you know that?" He rubs his thumb on my cheek bone.

Blushing, I bite my lip. He chuckles and kisses my forehead. Sighing, I drag myself off the bed. Looking into Arabella's bedroom I don't see her.

The sinking feeling of her going outside shoots through me. After checking every single room upstairs, I run downstairs, frantically looking around the living room.

Don't panic, Syd. She's just hiding somewhere: I tell myself as I walk into the kitchen. There she is. She's sitting at the counter holding a bowl and spoon. Ready to help me make breakfast. Once my heart rate returns back to normal, I walk over to her.

She looks up and her smile lights up her chubby face, her blue eyes shining bright. The cutest little dimples pop out on both cheeks. She has come so far. The first couple of days when we got her, Kane and I walked on egg shells afraid something would set her off. She would wake us up screaming. For two whole weeks she had nightmares and they finally just stopped completely. We don't find her in the closet anymore. I was so afraid that yesterday would set her back, but my strong baby girl is the same.

Someone is after me. I don't think about it as much as I should. Kane has this way about him that makes you feel safe no matter what. His presence just being close I feel whole and safe. Arabella feels the same thing. You can see it on her face how much she cares about that man. I also love him with all my heart and soul. Arabella is my daughter, but she is a daddy's girl all the way. Not that I blame her.

"Mommy, you gonna tome over?"

Arabella has her elbow propped up on the edge of the counter with a bored look on her face.

"Yes, love bug. I was thinking."

Walking over to the refrigerator, I open it and pull out ingredients for French toast.

"What you thinkin'?"

"About how much I love you and Daddy."

"Wuv you too, Momma," she says in her sweet baby voice. My heart melts as I set stuff on the counter. Kissing the top of her head, I begin putting all the ingredients into the bowl. Taking out some French bread, I begin cutting it in half.

Arabella dips the bread in the mixture, and I put it on the stove. I enjoy our special time together every morning.

Kane comes up behind me. I smell him before anything else. His arms wrap around me from behind. "Smells good," he tells me and runs his nose along my neck and cheek. Shivering, I flip the French toast.

He lets me go and turns to Arabella. "Good morning, beautiful." He kisses her cheek and picks her off the bar stool tickling her. Her giggling fills the room. It never gets old hearing her sweet giggles.

Kane sets her in her seat and helps me carry breakfast over to the table. Kane cuts up her food and pours some syrup on it for her. I melt every single time I see him take care of her.

Smiling, I dig into my food. Arabella slowly eats. Any creak or sudden movement still frightens her and she still tries to hide the food. When she looks around her and at us she relaxes.

Once everyone has finished eating I put everything in the dishwasher. Kane goes up stairs to fix our headboard. He may or may not have broken it last night. I heard it crack, but hey, I was in another world. I had a Bella and Edward moment. *Ha!*

An idea pops into my head. Grinning evilly, I turn to Arabella. "Let's play a trick on Daddy."

She starts jumping up and down. Taking her hand, I lead her up to her bedroom. Her top shelf in her closet is a stash of water balloons and guns. Grabbing the water gun, we sneak to her bathroom. I peek in on Kane; he's screwing something back onto the wall.

"Sweetheart, when Daddy comes in you have to spray him in the face with the water, okay?"

She giggles and nods her head. Turning around, I go to the hair dryer. Plugging it in, I take the baby powder and pour a good amount into the hair dryer.

Turning back to Arabella, I instruct, "When I say now you spray him in the face, okay?"

"Otay, Mommy."

"Ready?" She nods with a big grin on her face. She sets her face and stares straight ahead, ready for business. It takes all my willpower to keep from laughing at her.

"Kane, come here! The hair dryer won't work."

I can hear him move something around before I hear his footsteps heading in this direction. Making sure I'm standing by the plug so I can press the button, he steps into the room.

He takes the hairdryer from me and asks, "What's wrong with it?" Shrugging my shoulders, he looks down into the dryer. "Now," I tell Arabella.

She absolutely soaks him and he looks at her shocked. She giggles. Clicking the reset button on the plug, the dryer starts and covers him in baby powder. All you see is a white puff of powder that coats his face and neck. Only thing showing is his eyes open and his nostrils. Clutching my belly, I roll around on the ground. Arabella is lying beside me laughing.

"I'm giving you a thirty second head start! You better run before I catch ya." He then starts counting. "One!"

Arabella looks at me in panic. Taking her hand, I lift her off the ground. We run down to the steps as fast as we can. She giggles the whole way. We head straight outside. I can hear him yelling from inside the house just as we get to the barn. Taking a horse out of the stall, I lift Arabella onto it and then I step on a stool and jump on bareback. Kicking the house in the side gently, he takes off.

Kane walks in the barn just as we head out the other side. He laughs, and I can hear another set of horse hooves on the ground a few seconds later.

"Hurry, Mommy, he gonna get us," Arabella whispers

while looking over my shoulder.

She's sitting so her belly is against mine, her legs on top of my legs. She has her arms wrapped around my waist. My arm is wrapped around her to keep her steady.

"We got this, love bug." We go as fast as I will dare with Arabella riding with me. Looking back, I see Kane is coming up fast behind us.

"Oh, shit!" I whisper to myself. I know we are caught. Kane cleaned the baby powder off his face and has a new shirt on. He comes up beside us. Slowing down to a trot, Kane pretends to be mad at us both. Arabella knows this considering she has him wrapped around her little fingers.

"Hey, Daddy," she says in the sweetest little voice. Giving her an approving look, she giggles quietly.

"Hey, sweetheart." His face softens.

"I wike your white hair." She gives him a sweet smile. I laugh silently at his facial expression.

"I bet you do," he grunts out.

"Can I wide with you, Daddy?" *She's got him.*

"You sure can, baby girl."

I stop the horse and lift her off mine as Kane reaches for her. He leans over and whispers in my ear. "I'm going to spank your ass for that shit tonight." He bites my earlobe and turns back to Arabella. My whole body shivers. Maybe I should do this more often.

We take our time riding back to the barn, enjoying the morning sun. Closing my eyes, I smile because I'm incredibly happy. One hundred percent happy for the first time in my life. Life can only get better from here on out.

Leading my horse to Kane, I go straight into the house with Arabella. Kane comes in a few minutes later. SMACK! "Ouch!" I yelp and turn around to glare at Kane.

He's giving me a shit-eating grin. Rolling my eyes, I open the fridge to get a bottle of water and immediately gag. Putting my hand over my mouth, I run to the bathroom. Slamming the door behind me, I fall down to my knees, vomiting my breakfast into the toilet.

Hands pull my hair away from my face. A cold washcloth is placed on the back of my neck a second later. Letting out a ragged breath, I try to control my nausea. I feel immensely better, but still feel sick.

"Are you okay, baby?" Kane asks while rubbing my back soothingly.

I nod my head. I'm not ready to answer with words because I'm still queasy.

"Do you want me to carry you to bed?"

I shake my head no, but he doesn't listen. He lifts me off the cold floor and up into his arms. Laying my head against his chest, he carries me up to our room and gently lays me down onto the bed.

He smooths my hair away from my face lovingly, then leans down and grabs a throw blanket and tucks it under my chin.

"Rest," he tells me sternly.

"Okay," I whisper and close my eyes. Nothing is worse than having an upset stomach and throwing up. I was fine until I opened the refrigerator. The smell of different meats hit me in the face. I can gag at the thought. That's never happened to me before. Closing my eyes, I try to relax. Then it hits me like a freight train. My mom told me when she was pregnant that opening the refrigerator made her get sick every single time. She would have to plug her nose. I

can't be pregnant, right? *No way. I'm on the shot.* I must be getting the stomach flu. *But what if I am? What will Kane say? Arabella? Oh God, Arabella.* My poor baby girl. *What will she say? Will she be jealous?* I will love her just as much as any of my own kids. I'm scared.

Pushing off the bed, I walk to the night stand. My nausea long forgotten. I'm going to have Brae and Jessica pick me up and take me to get some pregnancy tests. I want Kane there, but I want to be alone to confirm it.

Grabbing my phone. I type out in a group message.

Me: Holy shit.

Brae: What's the matter? O.o

Jessica: Did you get a condom stuck up your vagina?

Brae: What the hell. Is that even possible?

Jessica: Oh it is! Hey, Sydney, are you okay?

Me: I need you guys to come pick me up.

Brae: What's the matter? Did Kane do something?

Jessica: Do I need my Taser? Because that bitch can fry dick.

Me: No, no, no. Nothing like that. I think I'm pregnant...

Brae: OH MY GOD! REALLY? I will be there thirty.

Jessica: I hope so, bitch. I won't be alone anymore. Brae pick my ass up first.

Brae: Be there soon, bitches.

Taking a shaky breath, I go in the bathroom to brush my teeth. As I go back downstairs my whole body shakes with nervousness and anticipation. I know Kane will be happy, but I'm worried about how Arabella will take it. I don't want her to think that I will abandon her or feel left out. That will *never* be the case.

Walking into the kitchen, I see Kane has Arabella up on the counter. Walking over to her, I pull her into tight hug. "You know how much I love you, don't you?"

"Wuv you, too." She lays her head on my shoulder. Feeling eyes on me, I look up to see Kane looking at me strangely.

"You're supposed to be in bed." He gives me the stink eye.

"I feel better. Brae and Jessica will be here in thirty. We're having a girls' day," I tell him nervously.

He nods but keeps looking at me strangely. I manage a reassuring smile, but on the inside I'm so nervous. Beyond nervous. A nervous breakdown would be more accurate.

"I'll keep Arabella with me. I'm going on a horse ride."

Nodding my head, I give him a kiss on the cheek. "Arabella, let's give you a bath." She nods, and I set her down on the floor. She takes off toward her room to get some toys to bath with. Before I can take one step, Kane grabs my hand.

"Are you sure you're okay?" He looks down at me concerned.

"Yes, love. I'm fine." I pat his cheek, and he gives me that smile. That perfect sideways grin.

Twenty minutes later, Arabella is bathed, and I'm slipping on some pants. I just straightened my hair slightly and brushed on some mascara. Looking in the mirror, I turn sideways to look at my belly. I know it's not possible to be showing, but it's very possible I could be pregnant. It's been over two months since Kane and I first had sex. *Thinking back, when was the last time I had a period? Wait. It's been before Kane and me had sex. Holy shit. How did I not know this?* Arabella came into my life, and I was consumed by her and Kane. It never crossed my mind.

I see a small bump. It's barely noticeable, but it's there. *Holy crap.* My hands go to my mouth at the sight. I have to be pregnant.

The doorbell rings, and I can hear Arabella's footsteps running to the door. Walking down the steps, Brae and Jessica look up at me with excitement. Rolling my eyes, I walk over to Kane who is watching me also.

"Love, if something is wrong, you can tell me." He looks at me really concerned, and I hate that look on his face. I just can't tell him unless I know for sure.

"I'm fine, baby. I love you." I stand up on my tippy-toes to kiss him. He meets me the rest of the way. He kisses me, but it's not a light peck like I originally thought it would be.

No, he mauls me, pulling at my hair and ass grabbing.

"Okay, guys, break it up. I don't mind the live porn, but your daughter might," Jessica interrupts us.

Pulling away, I look over at Arabella who is staring at us. Embarrassed, I look away. Kane rubs my rosy cheeks. "I will see you later, love." He presses a kiss on my forehead.

Turning to Arabella, I say, "I will be back later. I love you." I give her a quick hug.

"Wuv you too, mama."

"All right, bitches, let's get the show on the road," Jessica says while clapping her hands together.

"My daughter is over there. Can it." I point over my shoulder at Arabella as I pull my bag up higher on my shoulder.

She looks over at Arabella. "Sorry, Arabella."

"It's tay. I know not to say bitches." Her eyes widen.

That sets everyone off laughing. Kane picks her up off the ground and she wraps one arm around his neck.

Telling Kane bye again, we walk out to the car. As soon as we are all seated the first thing out of Jessica's mouth is, "Holy hell that was hot!" She fans herself. Laughing under my breath, I look out of the window at my house already missing Arabella. I haven't left her much over the past two days.

"That was pretty frigging hot. Now let's go see if you have a bun in the oven."

Nodding, I suddenly feel nauseous again. Placing my hand on my belly, I wonder: *Is there a baby in there?* The drive to the pharmacy flies by because I am so lost in my thoughts. I love Arabella and being her mom. I always wanted to be a mother.

Walking inside I grab five different pregnancy tests. After paying for them, I hurry to the bathroom. I try to get in alone, but my friends push their way in. Brae has a plastic cup.

Yeah, because I'm peeing in that.

"You're not going to watch me pee, are you?" I ask them, exasperated.

"Are you sick? We are going outside while you pee." Jessica gags and turns around while holding her belly.

Brae hands me the cup and walks outside while I pee. After I pee in the cup, I place the pregnancy tests in the cup. After lining them on the sink, I go to open the door.

The next five minutes are the longest five minutes ever. My phone timer goes off, and I look at Brae and Jessica. They both have anxious looks on their faces. Finally getting my legs to move to the sink, I grab the first one. Positive. The next. Positive. Every single one is positive. The last one is digital. Pregnant.

Handing them the digital one, I lean against the wall letting it all sink in. I have a baby in my stomach right now. A baby that Kane and I created together. Placing my hand on my belly, the tears start to fall. I always wanted to be a mother. Now I will be to two kids. I am so incredibly happy that I'm pregnant, but my worry is Arabella.

"Congratulations," Brae says. Jessica starts squealing.

"How are you going to tell Kane?"

"I don't even know."

"Do you want to go to a doctor to get an ultrasound?"

I nod my head and call my gynecologist's office. They can see me in an hour because of a cancellation.

Walking into the doctor's office, I fill out all the necessary forms. They make me pee in a cup again. The nurse comes in and confirms what I already knew. They draw my blood, check my blood pressure. Finally, the gynecologist comes in.

"Congratulations on the baby!" she says enthusiastically. I'm not able to keep the grin off my face. She keeps talking, but all I can see or think about is the big ass wand she's currently rolling a condom on.

Gulping, I watch as she comes over closer with it. "Today we're doing a vaginal ultrasound."

Letting out a deep breath, she lifts up my gown. I can hear the snap of the bottle. *Yeah, it's official…I'm freaking out.* She sticks in it. *Umm, yeah, that's uncomfortable.* Soon, the uncomfortable wand probing my vagina is forgotten. The sound of my baby's heart beat changes everything. Taking my phone out, I record it for Kane. The doctor has a strange look on her face, one that makes my stomach sink like I've just gone over the top of a rollercoaster.

Finally, she says, "Well, I believe I do hear another heartbeat." My own heart stops. *Twins?*

"What?" I ask her.

"You're having twins." She says with a huge grin.

"Twins." I repeat while gaping at her.

I can't stop the tears, putting my hand to my mouth I try

to hold back the sob that's trying to break free. I need to call Kane. Turning to the doctor I ask her, "Do you mind if I FaceTime my boyfriend."

She smiles and gives me the go ahead.

He answers after a few rings. "Hey, baby." His expression automatically changes once he sees the tears rolling down my face.

"Sydney, are you okay? What happened?" he asks frantically.

"I'm pregnant, Kane," I tell him, not able to keep the grin off of my face.

"What?" His face changes to shock.

"With twins," I whisper out next.

"Twins," he repeats then a big grin over comes over his face.

"Yes." I motion for the doctor to turn up the volume of the baby's heartbeat.

"Well I'll be damned. My boys can swim." He chuckles to himself.

Laughing out loud. "Hurry your ass home, woman. I need to hold you and my babies. Arabella is down for a nap."

Nodding my head, I tell him, "I love you."

"I love you too, sweetheart."

Ending the call, I see the doctor, Brae, and Jessica crying. "I love my job," the doctor tells me.

She gives me some papers, prenatal vitamins, and the time to come back in the next few weeks. I walk out of the doctor's office smiling from ear to ear.

fourteen

Brae pulls up in front of my house twenty minutes later. Kane rushes out of the house and down the steps. He all but rips my door open. He gently takes my hand and lifts me out of the car, his hands shaking as they go gently to my belly. He stares down at it for a second before his eyes meet mine. His eyes are so full of love that I feel it down to my soul.

"Baby, I had a big freaking proposal planned out. Brae and Jessica were helping me plan it. But now knowing that I put two kids in you I don't see a more perfect time to ask you this." He takes my left hand in his before getting down on one knee.

My heart stops. I can't believe this is happening. Putting my hand to my mouth in shock, I don't even look at the ring; I look at my man who's staring at me.

"The love I have for you, Sydney, consumes me. I love you so fucking much. Don't ever doubt that because what I feel for you is unwavering. I love everything about you. Your laugh, your smile that lights up the whole entire room, your heart. You're beautiful on the inside and out. The way you scrunch up your nose when you're annoyed. I will love, care, and protect you until my last breath. Will you marry me, Sydney, and be mine forever?"

Nodding my head, I scream, "Yes!" I pull him off the ground and wrap my arms and legs around him, hugging him to me as tight as I can. Pulling back, I kiss him. His hand comes to my jaw, pouring everything we feel into a kiss. I love this man.

"Mommy? Daddy?" I hear Arabella call out.

Pulling away, I look toward the house. Kane gently sets me down and walks over to her. "I have something for you, baby girl." He gets down on one knee before her like he did me. My heart melts at the sight.

"Will you do me the honor and let me be your daddy forever and ever?"

She grins and nods her head. He takes a necklace out of his back pocket and clasps it around her. "I love you so much, baby girl." He kisses her forehead and pulls back.

Her bottom lip trembles and he hugs her tightly to him. Her little shoulders shake as she cries onto his chest.

"Shhh, don't cry." She leans up and he kisses her tears away. If it's even possible, I just fell in love a little more with Kane.

Deciding to tell her now that she's going to be a sister,

I'm beyond nervous what her reaction will be. Getting down on my knees in front of her, I take a deep breath.

"Hey, sweetheart."

"Hi, Momma." She places her little hand on my cheek.

"Baby girl, you're going to be getting two brothers or sisters."

"I am?" Her little eyes widen.

"Yes, I have two babies growing in my tummy." I put my hand on my belly to show her.

My eyes never leave her.

She looks down at my belly sadly. "I wish I came from your tummy."

"Oh, sweetheart. It doesn't matter if you came from my belly or not. You're my baby. I love you just the same." I take her little hand in mine.

"Otay, Mommy. I want brothers." She giggles and wraps her arms around my neck.

"Me too. Help me keep those boys in line," Kane mumbles from behind me. I give him an annoyed look—only Kane would be thinking about stuff like that. It's hard to believe all this is happening so fast.

Arabella lets go and runs into the house. Standing, I look around at Kane. He is staring at me. "I can't believe I'm pregnant, Kane."

"I've cried enough today to last me a lifetime, you sappy fuckers. We're going to head out," Jessica says from behind us.

Turning around, I see black makeup running down their faces. I can only imagine what I look like. "All right, guys,

I will talk to you later." I walk over and give each of them a small hug.

Kane and I walk into the house hand and hand. He leads me over to the couch and sits down beside me. He smiles at me. "I am so fucking happy. We have a baby girl, I got a ring on your finger, and two babies in you. Life doesn't get better than this." He lifts my shirt up and gets on his knees. He leans forward and presses a kiss on my belly right below my belly button.

"I can't wait to meet you, babies. Daddy already loves you so much."

Holy shit. The dam is about to break. This day has been the best day of my whole entire life. It also hasn't quite sunk in yet. I was so scared that Arabella would be upset, but to my surprise, she wasn't. She was happy about it. I won't let her doubt for one minute how much I love her.

Pulling Kane up, I press a kiss on his lips. He grins against my lips. Pulling away, I prop my head on his shoulder.

"We're pregnant," I repeat again, still in shock.

"Yes, baby, we're pregnant." His chest moves with his laughter.

"Holy shit, you put a baby in me."

"Yes I did, not just one, but two." I can hear the cockiness in his voice. I guarantee he has the cocky smirk on his face, too.

"Two babies," I repeat. *I'm pregnant with twins.*

"They're going to be boys, I know it." He pinches the side of my butt cheek.

"Ouch, what did you do that for?" I smack his chest playfully.

"Because I wanted to." He gives me a wink and stands up. He scoops me off the couch and sets me down on the ground.

"Uhh, why did you pick me up like that and set me on the ground. Wouldn't it have been easier if you pulled me up?"

"Don't look at me like that. You're carrying precious cargo."

This will be a long pregnancy. Kane and his pestering was bad before, but now? *Yeah, I might as well get used to being bedridden.*

"I'm going to go buy some pregnancy books."

I watch as he practically runs out of the room. Laughing at his antics, I head upstairs to be with Arabella.

Throwing my head back, I moan as Kane sucks my clit. Opening my eyes, I see I *was* dreaming. Well, sort of.

Pushing him away and onto his back so I can pleasure him at the same time, I pull his boxers down. I take his dick in my hand and pump it twice. Licking all around the tip. Licking down his shaft and back up. Taking him as deep as I can while pumping my hand at the bottom. Swirling my tongue on the tip, I lick around the pre-cum. Taking him to the back of my throat, I swallow. His hips jerk at the movement, and he moans.

Moaning with his dick in my mouth, he slams into the back of my throat. Gagging, I stop him before relaxing my throat. He pumps his dick into my mouth. Hollowing my cheeks, I suck him as hard as I can and let go with a pop. Licking up and down his shaft again, I look up and his toes are curled.

He takes my hips and turns me around. "Ride my cock, baby."

Taking his dick, I place him at my entrance and slide down.

"Shit," Kane hisses.

Feeling powerful, I place my hand on his chest and slam up and down. He takes my hips and takes over. Laying partially down as he drives up in me, my breath is taken away, and I grit my teeth at the sensations.

His hand touches my clit, and I jump. It's too much. "Come now." He pinches my clit, and I explode. Crying out, he keeps pumping in me before he cries out his release moments later.

Out of breath, I lie on his chest. He rubs my back and plays with my hair. "That was great." I laugh sleepily at him.

"Yes it fucking was. Go back to sleep. It's 3 AM."

What the hell? The clock reads 3 AM, just like he said. Kane is staring at the ceiling with a grin on his face. I would be pissed, but that was a good freaking orgasm. Rolling over so my back is to him, he rests a hand on my belly, my back to his warm chest.

Kane

I slowly get off the bed and walk out of the room as Sydney sleeps. Walking over to Arabella's room, I find her sleeping cuddled up to her teddy bear. When she is sleeping, she has to be completely surrounded by things. Pillows, blankets, dolls, anything. She feels safe this way. I remember doing the same thing. Growing up with a parent who is on drugs is hell.

The fear, being always hungry, cold. The need to feel love. People constantly coming in and out. Not knowing who is going to hurt you and who won't. Trust isn't an easy thing. Arabella shocks the hell out of me. It took a little while for her to open and feel safe around us, but now she is a happy little girl. The sad thing is she will always bear the scars of what happened to her. She won't remember it, but she will feel it.

Pressing a kiss to her forehead, I tuck her in tighter. Placing the pillows on the end of the bed closer to her body, I close the door until there is a small crack. Going down the steps, I make sure every single window and door is locked.

Grabbing my guns from my many hiding places, I clean and reload them. Yesterday has me paranoid.

Three months ago, I met the love of my life in the worst possible circumstances. She became my rock, my healer, my everything. She healed me in so many ways. Being with her soothed me and my demons. Holding her keeps them at bay. Sydney doesn't deserve someone like me who is damaged, but I will do everything in my power to be worthy of her.

Replacing the guns back in their hiding spots after I clean them, I grab my truck keys and go to the back of the house where I keep my gun safe. Unlocking it, I grab my pistol and reload it. This is going by the bed in the nightstand where I have a secret compartment. Going up the stairs I look in on Arabella one last time before returning to my bedroom. I place my pistol safely in the gun compartment and after locking it up and triple checking it, I climb into bed. Pulling the blankets back, I roll Sydney over onto her back. Placing my hand on her belly, I rub in slow circles. It's hard to believe that there are two babies in there. Leaning forward, I press a kiss on her belly button. Lying on the bed, I tuck my head between her neck and shoulders with my arm holding her belly.

The doorbell ringing has me springing up in bed holding my chest. Kane jumps out of bed and goes downstairs. I grab Kane's shirt and run to Arabella's room who is sitting up in bed scared.

Arabella runs and grabs my hand. We walk down the stairs together. Going around the corner, there is a man who is the same height as Kane, but his shoulders are a little broader than Kane's. Kane hears our footsteps and looks back at us. That gives me sight of the man's face. Wow, he is ruggedly handsome. Bad boy with tattoos. Blushing, I look down at Arabella who is staring at him in wonderment.

She pulls her hand from mine and goes to Kane. She pokes him in the back. He looks down and she lifts her hands up for him to take her. He lifts her up and she lays her head on his chest. Walking over to Kane, he wraps his other arm around me and places his hand on my belly. The man standing before us looks completely shocked.

"Sydney, this is Isaac. Isaac, this is Sydney, my fiancée. This here is Arabella."

Giving the man a polite smile, he looks back and forth between us three.

"Isaac was in the military with your brother, Chase, and me. We own the construction business together."

"I remember," I tell him. "Nice to meet you." I give Isaac a polite smile. "I will go get started on breakfast." Getting on my tip-toes so I can give Kane a kiss, he leans down, kisses me, and sets Arabella down. She heads straight for the kitchen. Before I can even make a step Kane smacks me on the ass. Giving him the finger from over my head, I join Arabella.

When breakfast is ready, Arabella tugs at my shirt. That is when I realize I'm still in Kane's shirt without a bra. *Shit.*

"Mommy has to go change. We will get you dressed, too." We run up the stairs, and I slip on a bra and another t-shirt. After throwing my hair in a bun, I put a small bit of mascara on. Walking into Arabella's room, I see that she already has a dress on. Taking her hair, I give her a matching bun.

Kane and Isaac are still talking as we go back to the

kitchen. "Breakfast is ready."

They both get up and walk into the dining room. Kane gets his plate and grabs mine.

"Mommy, can I take Ieks?"

Nodding my head, I hand her his plate loaded with pancakes. I follow behind with syrup and butter. She sets the food on the table. Isaac looks down at her with a soft expression that causes her to blush. Grinning at her actions, I watch as she runs back into the kitchen and comes back with a glass. She hands it to Isaac.

"Thanks, sweetheart." She gives him a huge smile and then runs over to Kane. Grabbing Arabella's plate, I set it in front of her and she digs in.

We have a ritual: I cook, Kane cleans up. He grumbles about it, but does it without me asking. Arabella went upstairs to her room and Isaac went out to get his bag. Kane asked him if wanted to stay with us for a while until he buys a new house. His house burned down two days ago. Kane and Isaac are best friends. They met each other on the streets and joined the marines together. That's where they met my brother and Chase.

So lost in thought, I don't notice Kane coming up behind me until he lifts me off the ground and up onto the island. "Baby, seeing you bent over the counter like that has me so fucking hard." He takes my hand and presses it against his dick. "This is what you do to me all the fucking time. I want to bend you over this counter and fuck you so hard."

I gulp and try to control my breathing. *Holy shit, that was fucking hot.* Biting my lip, I moan under my breath. He growls and slams his mouth on mine. Dragging my fingernails up his abs, side, and then his back, his hand sinks in my hair and controls the kiss. Taking his hips, I pull him harder against me. Biting his lip hard and pulling. That causes him to smack my ass, and I moan.

Someone is walking around in the living room and that causes me to pull away. If I don't stop now, we won't be stopping. He rests his forehead on my shoulder while we both try to catch our breath.

He grabs my hips and lifts me down to the ground. Taking his hand in mine, I pull him to the living room so we can go and check on Arabella. Walking around the corner the sight before us has us stopping in our tracks. Arabella is sitting on the floor and Isaac is sitting in front of her. He has a tiara on his head and is cradling a doll in one arm.

He hears us walk into the room and his head whips around. "Don't say a fucking word."

That causes me to giggle and Kane has a knowing smirk on his face.

"Those big eyes and smile got me. Shit. I couldn't tell her no." He looks at Arabella who knows he's talking about her. She can't help it; she lays on the charm thick. She gives him her dimpled smile which causes Kane to laugh. She wraps anyone and everyone around her little finger.

"I'm going to lay out some steaks for dinner and go call the gang over to join us." Walking back to the kitchen, I know Kane is staring at my ass because he always does. He's an ass man.

The rest of the day is uneventful. Isaac plays with Arabella all day long. Kane is getting pissy because his baby girl is focused on someone else. The doorbell rings, and I walk to open it. Like always, Kane beats me there.

Brae walks in wearing a sundress and gives me a quick hug while packing the dish she brought. Jessica walks in holding her stomach which my hands gravitates to.

Chase and Ethan walk in next. Their gaze goes straight to Isaac's. They look shocked and then they both smile.

"Well, well, well. Nice to see you again, man," Chase says.

They do that hand smacking one arm thing. Ethan goes next.

"Kane, grill the steaks and burgers," I tell him.

He nods and lays a kiss on my forehead as he walks by. That causes me to blush because everyone is watching us. SMACK! Kane smacks my ass as he leaves. I jerk and let out a deep breath that causes my bangs to fly off my face. Everyone laughs.

The door opens again and in walks Mom and Dave. "Grandma!" Arabella yells and tackles her legs. She lets go and raises her arms up for the Sergeant to pick her up. He does and gives her a big grin. She pats his cheek and looks around.

Grabbing plates from the kitchen, I take them out on the patio. Kane is turning steaks over on the grill. Coming up from behind him, I spin a towel around and whip it at his butt hard. It makes a very satisfying smacking noise. The kind of noise where you know it hurts like a bitch. Snorting, I back up. Kane stiffens and turns around with a murderous glare. My eyes widen, and I take off running into the back yard.

Thinking I got away I look behind me, but I'm wrong. He is walking and is catching up to me it seems like. *What the hell? Is he freaking Jason?* Grabbing my tits, I run faster. I hate when my boobs move when I run.

Hands grabs my hips and lay me down on the ground. He tickles my sides. Squirming, I try to get him away from me. He starts laughing and that makes it worse.

"Okay, okay! I give up. If you don't quit, I'll pee on myself."

His eyes widen and then he lifts me off the ground. Dusting the grass off my butt, Kane attempts to help. What I mean by help is he just rubs my ass. Copping a feel.

"You better check the steaks." I smirk at him.

"Shit!" He takes off running to the grill.

Giggling to myself, I join the others who are watching us in amusement. Kane is eyeballing me, waiting to see if I get him again. Giving him a wink, I wag my fingers at him.

Before I know what's happening I'm thrown over a shoulder, and I look up at Kane in shock. His eyes widen and then turns pissed.

"Set her the fuck down! She's pregnant!" He charges over to Chase to beat his ass.

Hearing gasps all around us, I process Kane's words. Groaning, I cover my eyes while hanging upside down.

"Shit, man, I didn't know."

"Well don't do shit like that. Set her down if you want to see tomorrow."

He sets me gently on the ground, and Kane wraps his arms around me. "Are you okay?"

"I'm fine. I swear." I smile at him.

He nods and then I look over at the others who are staring at us in shock. My mom has tears in her eyes. Brae and Jessica just smirk.

"You're pregnant?"

Nodding my head, I place my hand on my belly. A sob escapes her and she runs over to me. Opening my arms, she hugs me softly.

"How far along are you?"

"I just found out yesterday. I'm having twins."

She gasps again and starts laughing. She turns to the rest of the crowd and yells at them, "They're having twins!"

"Kane, you have super swimmers," Chase tells him on a laugh.

Kane gives him a cocky smile while pulling me closer to him.

"Congrats, man." Ethan comes over and slaps him on the shoulder. "If you hurt my sister I'll kill you."

"Oh, one more thing! He asked me to marry him." I laugh out loud and their shocked expressions.

"Mommy!"

Looking around my mother, I see Arabella running toward me. When she steps in front of me, I ask, "What is it, sweetheart?"

"Der is a boy at the date. He wants to pway." Her little eyes are hopeful.

Looking over at Kane, I can't hide my confused expression. *What?*

"Let's go, sweetheart." Kane takes her hand.

She nods quickly and jumps up and down. Isaac and the rest of the men follow behind them which causes the rest of us to follow.

Walking through the house, I take a short cut. Walking up the winding driveway I see a little boy outside the gate that could be Arabella's twin.

"What the fuck?" Kane says shocked his expression mirroring mine.

The little boy flinches, but stares defiantly through the gate. He is older than Arabella. He looks around seven Kane opens the gate and the little boy steps through.

Kane bends down in front of him. "Who are you?"

"Her brother."

sixteen

"Her brother? Where are your parents? Your mom?" Kane asks him, softly.

"Dead. We have the same mom." He stares at the ground as he answers Kane.

Holy shit. How is this happening? What? When? How? Shaking my head in confusion, I walk forward so I am standing right beside Kane.

"Where's your dad?" I ask him softly.

His clothes are completely torn and dirty. His little cheeks are dirty. His hair overgrown. His eyes are like Arabella's when we got her—haunted and dull. Closing my eyes, I try to control my anger. Arabella is young and she will forget most things. He won't. He is old enough to remember a lot. His blue eyes stare directly in mine.

"My dad was in jail, but got killed there. The people that

were watching me dropped me off here as soon as they got a phone call this morning." He looks straight ahead showing no emotion. His little fists are clenched at his sides.

"Uhh, Kane, I was planning on telling you something. Can you come over here for a second? You too, Syd." Standing back up, I look at Ethan in confusion. Kane takes my hand and leads me over to Ethan. Just as we get closer to him I hear him mutter, "Is it possible that it can be linked?"

"Last night the man that tried to kidnap Syd was murdered by an inmate. From the rumors that were circulating, the gang he was in wanted him killed so he wouldn't rat." He looks over at the little boy in sympathy.

We are all that little boy has left. Kane walks off pissed. I follow after him knowing that we have to talk. He goes to the patio and sits down. He sees me and pats his lap. I sit down and snuggle close. Shocked, basically. My head can't wrap around this. The man, me, Arabella, that little boy?

"Sydney..." he starts. His eyes show nothing turmoil.

"I know, Kane," I whisper and look out at the field.

"We are all he has left. Arabella is his sister."

"I know. He has had such a hard life, Kane. You can see it in his eyes. Arabella had it bad, but she is young. He is older and will remember a whole lot more. Those big blue eyes will haunt me just like Arabella's did. They are filled with so much sadness and pain." My voice cracks at the last part.

"I know, sweetheart. I can't put him in foster care. What

kind of fucked up people would we be if we turned that little boy away?" he tells me sadly.

I nod my head in agreement. He takes a hold of my face and turns me around to look at him.

"Can you handle this, sweetheart?"

"I can handle anything with you by my side, Kane. Arabella is my daughter, and I love her so much. That little boy... I want to give him a good life too. He deserves it. He has no one. His mom overdosed. His dad was a mean and horrible person."

"He looks just like her." Her meaning Arabella.

"He really does."

I stand up and he takes my hand. Everyone is still standing there looking at each other. Arabella is standing beside the little boy holding his hand. Kane squeezes my hand tighter at the sight.

Kane pulls Ethan to the side to get everything sorted.

"Come on, everyone, let's go eat!" Clapping my hands, Arabella takes off running. The little boy stares at me in shock.

"What's the matter?" I ask softly not wanting to frighten him.

"You guys eat together?"

"Yes, we do." Smiling at him. "You hungry?"

He looks down at the ground ashamed. The growl I hear is proof enough. "Come on, let's get you fed."

I place my hand out for him to take. He looks at it warily then slowly places it in mine. Pulling his gently, we walk to the patio. Pulling out a chair for him, I grab a plate and load it with a steak and the works. Cutting up the steaks in little pieces for him, I set it in front of him and he just stares at it like Arabella did when she first came here. He then takes the fork and stuffs huge bites in his mouth. He eats and eats. Grabbing some water, I set it in front of him. He takes it and chugs it down. Hearing a sob, I look back to see Jessica and Brae crying.

Kane us a plate. Everyone is already eating. Arabella is sitting in Isaac's lap which makes me feel like a horrible mom—I forgot to get her a plate. "Don't worry I got her." Isaac nods his head at me. I give him a thankful smile.

The police show up a little while later with a social worker. He is to stay with us. He does have distant family, but they have many priors of drug abuse and the other is child neglect and endangerment. Carter is seven years old.

The man that attacked me when leaving the mall was his dad. Arabella and Carter have the same mom. Carter's dad was in the gang with my father. My mind is reeling at how connected it is. It's hard to believe. I didn't even know this town had a gang. Police records indicate that multiple cities in Texas have these gang members with the tattoo covering half of their face.

Standing in the living room once everyone is gone, I'm not sure what to do next.

"Kane," I call out.

"Yeah?" He peeks his head around the corner.

"He needs some night clothes and a spare outfit for tomorrow. Then I will take him shopping to let him pick out what he wants." He nods and smiles at me. He takes the keys from the hook and kisses me on the cheek before he leaves.

The couch is calling my name. This day has been exhausting and the police should just move in with us. They have been called so many times the past few months.

A giggling Arabella comes into the room pulling Carter who is looking around at the house in wonderment. His eyes connect with mine before falling back down to the ground. His body stiffens like he's afraid I'm about to scold him.

"Carter," I call him softly.

His head snaps to mine and slowly walks over. From his tense body you can tell he is scared. His movements are jerky as he moves toward me. His little hands are shaking. He sits on the corner of the seat and looks at the floor.

"I'm not going to hurt you, sweetheart." I slowly touch his shoulder. I want nothing more than to pull him into a hug.

"Promise?" His bottom lip is trembling as his tear-filled eyes meet mine.

"I swear. You'll never have to worry about that again." I move closer to him.

Tears run down his face. I raise my arms out in front of me knowing if I just hug him out right it will freak him out. He looks at my arms for a second and then throws himself into them. His little body is shaking from him crying so hard. Pulling him into my lap, he tucks his face in my neck.

"Mommy..." Arabella is watching us confused.

Placing a finger over my mouth, I let her know to be quiet. She runs off to go play. "Are you okay, honey?" I lean back slightly so I can see his face.

"You're not going to hurt me?" he barely manages to get out through the snubs.

"I would never ever hurt you. All I want is for you to be happy." I wipe my fingers under his eyes and dry his tears.

He starts sobbing again and my heart is breaking for this little boy. He cries onto my shoulder for a long time. He is still crying by the time Kane comes home. Kane watches us with clenched fists. Nodding my head toward the little boy, Kane nods and walks over to us.

He takes him from my arms and holds him close. Carter stiffens up and then wraps his arms around Kane's neck. "Carter, nobody will ever hurt you again, and I'll do everything in my power to make sure of that."

Carter nods his little head. He stops crying after few minutes. Kane just sways back and forth holding him.

"I'm going to get Arabella bathed. Can you help him?"

He nods and gives me a smile.

Walking into Arabella's room, I watch her play on the floor with her dolls.

"Come on, sweetheart. Bath time." I grab her pajamas out of the dresser.

As I'm combing her hair, Kane and Carter come in the room. I barely recognize him. Before he was covered in dirt, and now I can see that this little boy is absolutely gorgeous. He has dark blond hair that Kane must have cut. Arabella and he have the same colored eyes and he is really tall for his age.

I smile at him, and he looks down at the ground blushing. Kane gives me a wink.

"Tarter! You wook gweat!" Arabella jumps up and down, excited.

Laughing at her antics, Carter walks over and musses up her hair. Kane wraps his arms around me. We just watch them together. She has a brother. Kane's hand slowly slides down my back and to my ass, then he pinches it which causes me to yelp.

Smacking his chest, he laughs at me. Wrapping my arms around his neck, I look deep into his eyes. "I love you."

"I love you, too, sweetheart." Placing his lips on mine, he lifts me off the ground. My hands go to his hair. I almost forgot we had an audience. Hearing giggling, I lean back to see Arabella looking at us. Carter is staring at us shocked.

"Hop in bed, Arabella. I'll tell you a story. You want to stay too, Carter?"

He shakes his head no. "You want me to show you your

room?" He nods. "Kane, tell Arabella a story, and I'll go get him settled."

Walking out of the room, I go down the hall a few feet to the guest room. Soon-to-be Carter's new bedroom. "I will take you out tomorrow and you can pick out some things."

Pulling back the comforter and sheets, I wave him over and he slowly climbs into bed. He hugs the blanket close to his chest.

"Goodnight, sweetheart." I lean down and give him a kiss on the forehead.

"Night," he whispers.

Walking out of the bedroom, I feel defeated. It will get better like it did with Arabella, but there is nothing worse than feeling helpless. Peeking in on Kane and Arabella, who is already asleep, I see Kane checking her window.

Bracing my hip at the door frame, Kane takes my hand and we both walk down the stairs. Isaac is sitting on the couch and looks at us as we walk down the stairs.

"Is he okay?" Isaac asks

"I think he eventually will be," I sigh as I sink into the couch. Kane sits down and pulls me into his lap.

"He will be. He is strong," Kane says while rubbing my arm soothingly.

"He has seen a lot of rough things. He will always remember them, but he is lucky that he has you guys. Growing up, we didn't have that." He motions between himself and Kane. "That little boy will be getting more love than he can handle. It pours off you guys with Arabella.

The love you guys have for each other is strong. Just by watching you, people can see it."

I look at Isaac, shocked. I don't even what to say. What can you say to that? Kane grips me tighter to him, and I can tell he feels the same way.

"He has cigarette burns on his shoulder," Kane tells us solemnly

Covering my hands with my face, I growl angrily.

"Those stupid fuckers," Isaac grounds out between his teeth.

"You ready for bed?" I ask Kane, ready to get this day over with.

"Yeah let's go shower first." He winks and lifts me off his lap.

Walking ahead of him, he slaps my ass as I run up the stairs. *Yeah, shower sex is the best.*

Stripping my clothes off before I even make it in the bathroom, Kane is chuckling behind me at my antics.

Turning the shower on, I watch as Kane takes his clothes off. Looking down, I rub my belly. I had forgotten that I am pregnant and with twins at that. Smiling, I step into the warm shower. Kane comes in behind me.

Kane closes the distance between us, slamming his mouth onto mine as his hand snakes between my legs and he touches my bundle of nerves. Biting my lip, I lean my head back against the wall. He slips two fingers in me while his thumb circles my clit. He curls his fingers and hits that spot in me that has my toes curling. Moving my hips against his hand, I try to get more of anything.

"Kane, fuck me."

He smacks my ass and that has my thighs clenching together. *Holy shit.*

He lifts me off the ground and my legs wrap around him. My back presses against the cold tile.

"Hang on," he grounds out before he slams home.

Throwing my head back, I cry out while he pounds into me. With me braced against the wall in a way that I'm not moving, I claw his back as he swivels his hips and he hits that spot again.

"Harder."

He pounds impossibly faster. The fire spreading through me is almost too much.

"Come, baby." He circles my clit, and I explode. Kane pumps a few more times before he grunts out his release. Laying my head on his shoulder, I attempt to catch my breath. Kane gently unwinds my legs from his waist putting me back on the ground.

He grabs my bath sponge and then gently washes me. He shows me every day how loving and caring he is. Grabbing his face between my hands, I ask him, "What did I ever do to deserve someone like you? I love you with all my heart and soul, Kane."

I hug him and rest my head on his chest. His hand presses my head tighter to him. "I love you, too, sweetheart. More than my life itself."

He gets down onto his knees and presses a kiss to my belly. "Daddy loves you, too, my boys."

seventeen

Rolling over in bed I look over at the clock. 9 AM. Groaning, I slide out of bed and walk to the closet. I'm surprised Arabella isn't awake yet. Kane starts making the bed. Slipping on a sundress, I put some eyeliner and mascara on. Taking some powder, I pat it on my cheeks. SMACK! I jump as Kane gropes my ass as he walks to the other sink. "Will you knock that off?"

Kane puts his fingers to his chin in thought for a moment before grinning wickedly. "Never."

Rolling my eyes, I walk into Carter's room to check on him and as I get over to the bed, I see that Arabella has got into bed with Carter. He has his arm wrapped around her

LeAnn Ashers

protectively.

Walking back out of the room, I go back to our bathroom. "Kane, come here."

I stick my head in and run back, grabbing my phone off the table as I do.

After snapping a couple pictures of them, Kane walks into the room. "Look how cute, Kane!"

He chuckles at me and walks over to wake them up. Carter jumps up and moves in front of Arabella who wakes up sleepily, rubbing her eyes. She looks around confused.

"I'm not going to hurt you or Arabella," Kane tells him softly. Carter swallows and then slides off the bed. He looks up at Kane defiantly.

"All right, kiddos. I'm going to start breakfast. You can go downstairs to watch TV, play, or whatever." Arabella jumps off the bed and runs downstairs. I know she is heading straight for the kitchen.

I ruffle Carters hair as I walk past.

After breakfast is ready, I set Carter's plate in front of him and he stares down at it for a second and then up at me. Arabella carries Isaac's plate.

"Dig in, sweetheart." I ruffle his hair again.

He looks up at me and smiles. Smiles. That smile just made me fall in love with this little boy. He has those sweet little dimples that Arabella has. Kissing him on the forehead, I walk back to the kitchen. I can hear Kane coming up behind me. He wraps his arms around me from behind and lays his chin on my shoulder.

"He's going to be okay, sweetheart." He presses a kiss

on the side of my neck.

The rest of the meal is uneventful. Taking Arabella upstairs, I get her ready for the day. She wants to match me so she grabs her own little sundress. Carter and Kane walk in a minute later and they're matching in dark jeans a white t-shirt.

"*Oh my God*! Look at you guys!" I can't keep the squeal out of my voice.

Carter blushes and looks down at the ground. Kane smirks and stalks over to me giving me a kiss. Taking my hand, he leads me downstairs with the kids following behind us. Sneaking a peek back at them, I love how Carter's hair is gelled to the side. The urge to pinch his cheeks is becoming too much. He catches me looking and rolls his eyes.

Kane smacks my butt. "Leave him alone." My butt is sore enough from all the ass smacking, so I pull my hand back and smack him back hard. He yelps and gets that evil glint in his eye.

I hear giggling, and I look back just in time to catch Arabella pantsing her brother. My eyes all but fall out of my head.

I watch in shock as Carter starts laughing and that sets off the rest of us. Wiping my tears, I ask her, "Where did you learn that?"

"Chase!" she squeals and runs down the stairs. It puts me in full panic mode because I can see her falling down the steps and getting a concussion.

"Chase is a troublemaker," I mutter to myself.

"Says the person who put baby powder in the hair dryer." He takes a piece of my hair and gentle pulls it while smirking at me. I roll my eyes at him, but that doesn't stop me from grinning.

When we arrive at the store, I grab Carter's hand and lead him inside. Kane goes to pick out furniture. I go to the stuff he wants to decorate his room.

"All right how do you want your room decorated?"

He is staring at me like I have two heads.

Placing my hand on his back, I encourage, "Choose what you want, sweetheart."

He smiles at me and then walks off ahead of me. He walks down the aisle and stops at a dark blue comforter. He points at it and smiles at me. His little dimple pops out, and I want to squeeze him again. His eyes narrow like he knows what I'm thinking.

Pressing my lips together, I resist the urge not to smile and tackle him into a hug. He places his hands in front of him, but I grab them and pull him into me. He starts squirming, and when I let go he looks down at the ground blushing. Giggling at him, he looks up and glares at me. Twisting around, I make a big show of looking at the items on the shelves.

Kane pops around the corner with a buggy. Arabella sitting in the front basket. Grabbing the correct size comforter, he wants, I lay it in the buggy. "All right, sweetheart, let's pick out the rest of your things.

The things he picked out didn't match, but he wanted it so it's his. We go to the mall to get clothes and Kane will be taking him around to look at things he might want. Arabella will be staying with me because she loves clothes shopping as much as I do.

We go around the store getting pants, dress shirts, t-shirts, shorts, swimsuits, shoes and pajamas. The buggy is loaded full of clothes by the time Kane and Carter come back. Carter is grinning from ear to ear and is carrying a bag.

Looking at them curiously, Kane winks and pulls Carter closer to him.

Kane

Carter is acting all shy now that we are away from Sydney. He keeps peeking up at me and looks back down at the floor. He stops, and I look back to see him staring into a sporting goods store. He looks at me and then walks back over, but keeps looking back at the store staring at something.

"You want to go in there?"

He looks at me and then looks unsure what to say. So I just put my hand on his shoulder and lead him over to the store. "What do you want?" He looks so uneasy. "You don't have to be afraid, especially around me." He visibly relaxes and walks over to a pair of UFC fighting gloves. "You know what those are for?"

He nods. "I watched them fight on TV. I want to be able to fight like that. Nobody will mess with me again."

I don't blame him. As a kid all I wanted was to feel safe

and be able to take care of myself. I could fight at a young age, but it was street fighting. I still defended myself. If he wants to learn to fight, who I am to stop him? He will be trained, though. When I look at this little boy, I see so much of myself in him.

"Do you want to learn how to fight like that?" He grins and nods enthusiastically. "You will have to train and it won't be easy. I have a gym that teaches mixed martial arts. Do you want to go?"

"Yes!" He fist pumps the air. Chuckling at him, I grab a pair of kid gloves for him.

"I will call and ask when classes start. School starts in two days."

Paying for the gloves, I hand them to Carter who hugs them to him. The grin that comes over his face never leaves. Going back to the store where Syd is almost done with shopping, I walk inside to see her standing at the counter with a cart full of clothes.

Her face lights up when she sees us. Her smiling like that almost always puts me on my ass. She's so beautiful, and she is my fiancée. She is an amazing mother to our children, and she loves me. *Loves me.* It's hard to believe someone who is so honest and beautiful would want someone like me. I'm a selfish fucker, and I want to keep her.

Paying for the stuff, I grab all the bags. *How in the fuck am I supposed to carry this much?* By the time I make it to the truck I'm pretty sure my arms are going to fall off. The little straps of the bags cut into your skin. All but throwing the stuff in the truck, Carter hands me the other bags.

Picking up my baby girl, I set her in her seat and buckle her in. She pinches my nose.

"Ouch!" I yelp at her. She starts giggling and does it again. I place a kiss on her forehead and walk over to put Syd in the truck. Carter manages to get in himself. Syd gives me that sexy little grin that makes my limp dick hard in seconds. She looks down at my hard dick and smirks at me. She bites her lips.

"Tease me anymore, and I'll spank your ass later for that shit." I tap her ass lightly in warning.

"Oh, baby, I'm hoping so." She bites my earlobe and pecks my lips. Lifting her in the truck, I discreetly adjust my pants and jump in the driver's side. That girl will be that death of me.

Sydney

The next two days are filled with getting Carter settled in and then it's the morning school starts. While I'm getting his lunch ready, the cat rubs around my legs. I think back to the day before where Arabella brought him in the house with a big grin on her face.

"Momma, wook what I got." She hugs the cat to her and it wiggles, wanting down.

"I see that, baby." I bend down closer to her.

"Tan I keep it?" She gives me those big doe eyes.

"Ask your father about that." She grins because she knows she will get her way.

LeAnn Ashers

"Daddddy!" she yells in a sing-song voice.

He charges into the room frantic when he hears her yelling, but stops in his tracks when he sees her with the cat in her arms.

"What's that?" He points at the cat.

"It's a pussytat, Daddy." She rolls her eyes and looks down at the cat.

"Why is it here?" He looks at me accusingly. Shaking my head, I point to her.

"Oh, Daddy, tan I keep it? Pwease?" She evens looks like she is almost in tears. *Yeah, she's good.*

"Arabella, you don't need a cat," he tries to argue.

"Daddy, I always wanted a pussytat." Her bottom lip trembles.

"Okay, fine." He sighs and presses a kiss on the top of her head. She runs off squealing. I laugh at how hooked she has him. She just has to give him those eyes and he will agree to anything.

Kane walks past me to the fridge. Carter climbs up on the bar stool and eats his breakfast. Arabella is laying on the couch watching cartoons. SMACK! "Good morning, sweetheart. Your mother is taking Arabella for the day." He leans closer so he is almost whispering,

"When we get home I'm going to eat your pussy and fuck you all day." He kisses my cheek and stalks off. I clench my legs together in anticipation.

We drop Carter off at school. He walks into his classroom looking all cute. His seat is beside a girl and she smiles at him all sweet. He's too young for that shit. She

214

needs to keep her eyes to herself.

"Calm down, Momma Bear," Kane whispers into my ear. Laughing, I push Kane away. Walking over to Carter, I smother him with kisses.

He pushes me away and laughs out, "Stop, Mom."

My mouth falls open when I hear him call me Mom. His eyes widen then he looks down at the desk embarrassed. Leaning down so I can whisper into his ear, I tell him, "Don't be ashamed about that. I want nothing more than to be your Mom." I kiss his cheek and stand up. Kane takes my hand and leads me out of the room. We leave with one last glance at Carter.

The whole ride home I worry about him. Kane hurries over to my side of the vehicle when we arrive. I laugh at his antics as he pulls me into the house.

Lying in bed after three rounds of hot monkey sex, the phone starts ringing. Kane rolls out of bed and picks it up. His face changes and then looks confused. He runs downstairs.

Rushing after him confused, I see Kane looking everywhere for something.

"What is it, Kane? You're scaring me!" I yell at him.

"All right we will be there in thirty." He hangs up and looks at me.

"What is it, Kane? I swear if you don't tell me…" I charge over to him.

"Carter brought the cat to school with him today. It was in his backpack. It started meowing and the teacher came over to investigate."

My mouth falls to the floor. "Why?"

"I don't know." Kane lets out a deep breath and rubs a hand through his hair.

We hurry and get dressed. Racing to the school, we see Carter is sitting in the principal's office looking upset. The principal spots us and waves us in. She is an older lady around fifty or so. She points down to the seats beside Carter who has the cat in his lap still.

"Carter, since your parents are here, will you tell me now why you brought the cat to school? You did know it wasn't allowed, right?" the principal asks him.

He nods his head while looking at the ground still.

"Sweetheart, why did you bring it to school?" I put my hand on his face and tip his chin up.

"Because he—" he points at Kane "—said to you that he was going to eat your pussy! I didn't want Arabella to be upset!" he cries out and holds the cat tighter to him.

I blush from my head to my toes. We all stare at him speechless. The principal is looking at us wide-eyed then busts out laughing. Kane bends over and laughs his ass off.

"Carter, he wasn't going to eat the cat." I blush again and look up at the ceiling.

"He said so!" He stomps his foot on the ground.

"I think it's time for you to go back to class," the principal tells Carter. She gets up and tells her secretary to walk him to class.

"Oh my God!" I hiss at Kane while putting my hands over my face once the principal leaves the room. I wish the ground would swallow me up right now and hide me forever. It's the first day of school. It's freaking hilarious, and I'm sure I will laugh at this later, but Carter just told the principal that Kane was going to eat my pussy.

She sits down in front of us. "Well, I wasn't expecting that." She sighs and shuffles papers around on her desk.

"I'm so sorry about that!" I cry out to her.

I grab Kane's hand because I'm about to run out the door. I can feel Kane laughing beside me. I glare at him and that just makes him laugh harder. "I swear if you don't hush I will dismember you." His eyes widen and he turns to the side while holding his junk.

The principal is grinning at us. "All right, you guys can go home." I get up quickly and scoop up the cat. I speed walk out of the school. I stand outside of the passenger side of the truck waiting on Kane.

He opens the door and lifts me inside. Pulling down the mirror, I look at myself. My hair looks like a rats nest. Great, I even look the part. Kane notices what I'm doing and bursts out laughing again. I'm going to kill him.

Picking up a shoe off of the floorboard, I throw it and it bounces off the side of his head. His mouths pops open and then he starts laughing again. Flipping him the bird, I look out of the window the whole time he drives us to go pick up Arabella. Leaving her for the few hours we did earlier was long enough.

Feeling a hand on mine, I look over to see that we have stopped and we are parked outside of my mom's house. I was so lost in thought that I didn't even notice. Kane lifts my hand and kisses my ring finger.

"What are you thinking about, sweetheart?"

Pushing a piece of my hair behind my ear. "I was thinking about us. How five months ago we weren't even together, and now we are engaged and have kids. Since I have you I don't know what I would do if I ever lost you."

"Sweetheart, you are not going to lose me. You're stuck with me." He presses a tender kiss to my lips. Wrapping his arms around me, he whispers into my ear everything that he loves about me and our life.

Hearing squealing, I look up to see Dave and Arabella standing on the porch. Arabella is jumping up and down looking at us. Looks like someone is excited to see us. Kane drags me out his side of the truck and sets me down.

Arabella runs off the porch and tackles me with a hug. She acts like she hasn't seen us in days let alone a few hours.

"Did you have fun with Grandma and Grandpa?" I bend down to her level.

"Yes! We tolored and pwayed. Me and pop pwayed dress up! He was a pwincess and he was dorgeous." She jumps up and down while moving her arms enthusiastically.

Looking up at David who is staring down at Arabella like she has betrayed him, Kane lifts her off the ground and bites at her belly. That causes her to break out in a fit of giggles. Grinning at them, I walk into the house to see Mom cleaning up the kitchen.

"How was your morning?" She smirks at me.

"It went well." I cough, trying to hide my

embarrassment.

"Why are you back so early?" She gives me a curious look.

The reason why runs into the kitchen. *Oh no, I hope she doesn't ask why—*

"Why is the cat here?"

"Umm, Carter took him to school with him today," I barely whisper, hoping she won't hear.

She gasps and stares at me like I'm crazy. "What? Why did he do that?"

"Because he thought Kane was going to eat it."

"What? No!" Her head tilts to the side and stares at me confused.

"Yes, Mom," I groan and cover my face.

"There is more to the story than that." She gives me that motherly look that always has me spilling my guts.

"He heard Kane says he was going to eat my... Umm. Yeah." I point down to the location. Her eyes widen and then she bursts out laughing. She holds her belly. Not able to hold it in, I start laughing too.

"That's hilarious!" She wipes at her eyes.

Kane walks in with a smirk because he knows why we're laughing. Dave comes in behind him and he looks back and forth between me and my mom. She is holding her stomach.

"What is it?" he asks and walks over to wrap his arms around my mother.

"Carter took the cat to school today. He thought Kane was going to eat the cat. I'm assuming Kane said pussy?"

Dave stares up at Kane and then at me with wide eyes. *Oh God.* I groan as a huge smile overcomes his face. He walks back over to Kane and smacks him on the shoulder. Rolling my eyes at them, I go in the living room to put Arabella's shoes on.

Looking at my phone I see that it's 2:30 and we need to go pick up Carter. "Kane, we need to go get Carter!" I yell at him while slipping on my shoes and walking out to the truck.

Kane walks outside a minute later and buckles Arabella in and then helps me up. It sucks being short. For one, sex is awkward sometimes. If he fucks you over the table your feet will be hanging off the ground. Kissing while standing on the ground is a pain in the ass.

My phone goes off and I lift my butt up so I can get it out of my back pocket. I see that I have a text from Jessica.

Jessica: Where are you?

Me: Picking up Carter. What's up?

Jessica: Just checking in.

Me: Spill.

Jessica: I got me some D.

Me: OMG! Who? What? Where?

Jessica: Chase! We had a date and hit it off.

Me: Get it girl.

Jessica: Oh I did and much more. ;)

Me: We are pulling up at the school. Talk to you later.

Putting my phone down, we park along the sidewalk where the teachers lead the kids out. Carter is in second grade he is first. He is talking to another little boy. Kane jumps out of the truck and comes over to help me out.

Stepping up to the sidewalk, Carter's face lights up when he sees us. He points at us then tells the little boy something. Carter takes off running and then tackles me in a hug. Startled, I look up at Kane and then I hug him back.

"How was school today sweetheart?" I rub his cheek.

"I had fun. Missed you." He hugs me tighter and my throat feels thick. This sweet boy is coming out of his shell. Carter pulls back and hugs Kane's legs.

"Missed you too," he whispers.

"Missed you too, son," Kane leans down and hugs him tightly.

"What 'bout me?" Arabella asks him while stomping her foot.

"Missed you to Bell." He ruffles her hair before turning back to look at Kane again. "Do I get to go train now?"

"I just got the phone call this morning. You get to start next week." Kane ruffles his hair.

Carter looks down at the ground. "Okay."

"But tomorrow we get to get your gear."

"Yes!" He fist pumps the air and runs to the truck. Waiting by the door he is practically jumping up and down.

"Come on, Momma. Let's get you guys home." He leads me over to the truck and helps me in. Pressing a kiss on my lips, he shuts the door and helps Carter in.

eighteen

Today is the first day I have been out on my own. Completely alone. I wanted to take my time, buy some clothes for me and the kids. A baby bump popped up out of nowhere.

Walking outside of the mall, Kane calls, and I pick it up. "Hello?"

"Hey, baby. You on your way home? You snuck off on me," he says angrily into the phone.

"I'm sorry." I sigh into the phone. "I'm on my way home now. I love you." *I'm fucking stupid for sneaking off.*

After hanging up I stick my phone in my bra. Opening my car door, I never make it inside. Something slams against the back of my head. My face hits the glass of my car window and something cracks, then there's nothing but darkness.

Groaning, I turn over trying to get away, thinking about my children and my Kane. My two babies growing in my stomach. *Oh God, my babies.* Clutching my babies, I look up at my attacker. Gasping. *No. No way. This can't be.* Gasping for air, nothing comes out before his slams his foot down on my face.

There is a deep throbbing in my forehead and my throat feels like sandpaper. My body is like Jell-O. It's like I am having an out of body experience. I know what's going on around me but I can't control my body. My shoulder blade and arms are on fire. My head feels like fifty pounds, and I try to move my feet, but they barely move.

Hearing whimpering from beside me gives me enough strength to crack my swollen eyes open. Craning my neck to the side I see a naked woman whose arms are over her head. Blood is covering her back and legs. My heart stops when I realize where I am.

Cameron. I used to go to college with him. He was a stalker, basically. I turned him down because I was concentrating on my studies. He wouldn't take no for an answer. Everywhere I went, he was there.

The night when I finally had enough, I was walking home from work, and I could feel a presence behind me, and I knew instantly who it was. He followed behind not speaking or anything. Just following. I remember feeling the unease of what was happening.

Then his hand wrapped around my arms and he pushed them over my head. His eyes were coal black, and I will never forget feeling the fear of being helpless. Luckily, a police officer drove by at that time and he was arrested. I forgot all about him, but I never forgot the look he gave me as he was driven away in the police car or the bone chilling smile he gave me.

"Are you okay?"

Snapping out of my thoughts I look over at the girl. Her voice has to be the sweetest voice I have ever heard. "I'm okay, but are you okay?" I wince when I ask that because she isn't okay.

"I've been better. What did you do to get down here?" she managed out through her ragged breaths.

"Cameron... I went to school with him and—" I start, but I'm interrupted when I see him walk in with a sinister look on his face.

"Well well well. She is awake. Now, how should we start your torture, huh?" He tisks and trails a finger down my belly. My thoughts instantly going to my babies. Please God, someone find me.

Cameron picks up a knife and walks over me. Gulping I try to control my shaking body. He presses the tip on my chest. Wincing when he presses harder. His pupils dilate.

He's getting off on this. Vomit crawls up my throat.

Gun shots rang through the house. Kane. He's here. I can feel it. Cameron looks at me pissed off and then runs up the stairs. Dropping the knife as he goes.

Kane

When Sydney never comes home I snapped into action calling Ethan, Isaac, Chase, and Dave. Grabbing my keys, I walk downstairs to the basement. I go to the gun safe. Pressing in the code, I swing open the door and I take in my large assembly of weapons. Grabbing my AK and a load of weapons I make my way upstairs just as I hear vehicles roaring up my driveway.

Before I can make it out of the kitchen the door is slammed open and in runs Ethan. The rest of the guys are right behind him.

"What happened?" Ethan asks with a murderous look on his face.

"Your sister snuck off without me. She was supposed to be home an hour ago. She isn't answering her phone, and I have a feeling in my gut something has happened. I just need to figure out where she's at." Slamming my hands on the table, I'm ready to murder someone.

"Check the motherfucking tracking thing on her phone!" Ethan roars in my face. Pushing him back, I run to grab my laptop. Logging on, I see she is on the outskirts of town. I look at the men behind me. They have fought beside me, protected me as I did them. My brothers.

"I'm getting my fiancée. I'm not asking you to go with me, but that woman is my everything. The thought of her or my babies hurt is driving me crazy. I'm about to go kill some motherfuckers too. You never mess with what's mine, and that woman is *mine!*"

Grabbing my gun, I load it and some clips. When I hear guns clicking beside me I see the men beside me loading up guns. Smacking them on the shoulder, I pick up my phone to call Syd's mom to pick up Carter. Arabella is already over at her house because I was searching for Syd all day long.

Thinking of her has me punching the wall. I love her so fucking much. My heart is hurting from the being separated. Her smile that can make that meanest motherfucker smile. That woman has changed my life, and I'm going to get her back no matter what. Those men are going to pay. With their life.

Walking back into the kitchen, I see that all the men are ready. Their expressions show that they're ready.

"You guys don't have to do this." I cross my arms over my chest.

"We know we don't, but you have saved all of our lives more than once. Syd is my sister, and we all care about her." Ethan smacks my shoulder and the rest of the men nod their heads in agreement.

"Let's go." I walk out the front door and jump into my truck. They climb in and Isaac is sitting beside me giving me directions. Besides Isaac talking, there isn't any sound. We sit in silence because the shit that's about to go down can kill us all, but I'm not going down until my woman is safe.

We are a few miles away from the location when the roar of motorcycles is coming up from behind us. The one in front is waving for me to pull over. Shaking my head, I ignore them because my woman is close.

He smacks my window. Growling, I pull over and jump out ready to knock some motherfuckers out. The dude in the front slides off the motorcycle. His arms are covered in tattoos, and he is a mean motherfucker—I can see that from here.

Walking up to him, I stand nose to nose. "What the fuck do you want?"

He grins at me. "I'm about to kill some motherfuckers in that building up ahead. They've been kidnapping women and selling them. We are taking the fuckers out. Nobody messes with people in my town especially women."

Stepping back, I look at all of them. "My woman is in there. I'm going in to get her back."

"Let's get her back then. Follow behind us." He gives me a sinister smile and gets back on his motorcycle.

Jumping in I start the truck. "We got your back, man. We will get her back," Chase says.

Staring straight ahead, I prepare myself for what's to come. If one of them has hurt her I will kill all those motherfuckers. Clenching the steering wheel, I speed up as the motorcycle gang speeds up. The building is just up ahead.

They don't stop until they are right at the door. They jump off their motorcycles and run in.

"Let's do this shit."

Grabbing my gun, I run in the building. I can hear them right behind me. Walking inside, nobody is around. Then I hear gun shots. My body stiffens and my heart is pounding out of my chest. Taking slow breaths, I get into combat mode. Looking at the men behind me, they have the same expressions on their face. Nodding my head at them to see if they are ready, they nod back. Taking a deep breath, I pull my gun up and walk around the corner. We clear all the rooms and she isn't here.

My heart pounds into my chest as each room we clear doesn't produce Sydney. Going into the kitchen, I see three men on their knees and the MC dudes surrounding them. I point at the door that leads to the basement to one of those men. He nods and moves out of the way, but he follows close behind us. Five sets of footsteps follow behind me.

She better be fucking okay. Walking down the steps, my heart is beating out of my chest, but it doesn't prepare me for what I see. My woman's face is bloody, and she is hanging off the ground by her arms. Her blue eyes meet mine, and I run to her.

Looking over, I see a naked woman whose entire back is bloody and torn to shit. I've seen beatings like that before, and I know her back will be completely covered In scars no matter how well she heals. Averting my eyes because I can't stand someone hurt like that, I walk over to Sydney who is watching me. Removing the chains from her arms, she immediately starts to fall. She cries out as her arms fall to her sides. Picking her up bridal style, I look over to see Isaac helping the other woman down.

"Kane," Sydney groans.

Gripping her tighter to me, I run up the steps and into the kitchen, being careful not to jolt her too much. "Baby, which one of the men did this to you?" I look down at her swollen face ready to commit murder.

Three men are on their knees still. One is staring at Sydney with pure malice. Eyeing him, I know it's him. Sydney points at him and confirms what I thought. "You're mine," I mouth at him and walk out of the room. Ethan is close behind me.

"Take her, man, and get her to the hospital. I got business to take care of," I tell Ethan.

"Our prospect will drive you and the other girls to the hospital." The president walks up beside us and motions to the van.

A van pulls up beside us. Sydney is staring up at me and my heart is breaking from how her face looks. I don't want to leave her, but I have to make these men suffer.

"Kane, make him pay for what he did to the other girl," she barely manages to croak and squirms wanting down. Shaking my head no, I place her in Ethan's arms. "I love you, sweetheart I will be right behind you guys." I kiss her forehead.

"Love you," she whispers and cuddles into Ethan's chest. Isaac is coming out next carrying the other chick wrapped in his shirt now. He gives me a look that tells me to make sure he pays. The motherfucker isn't going to die easy.

"Let's kill some motherfuckers." The President gives me a look and walks into the kitchen. Passing the already dead body of Sydney's father in the living room with a gunshot right between the eyes.

Following behind him my eyes instantly go to the man who kidnapped and hurt my woman. *What kind of fucking man hits a woman?* I understand if she was beating the shit out of you for no reason and you push her off, but physically hitting her to cause hurt? That's uncalled for. Men are protectors, not abusers, and I'm about to cause this man a lot of fucking pain.

Walking up to the man, I lift him off the ground by his hair. Pushing him in the chair, I tie his hands behind his back. Taking a pair of brass knuckles from my back pocket. The man smiles at me. Fucking *smiles*. Rearing my hand back, I hit him twice. Blood and teeth fly out of his mouth.

Taking his hair, I pull his head back. "Tell me why you did all this? Her dad and that one sick fuck already in jail?"

His chuckles. Blood pours out of his toothless mouth. "Like I would fucking tell you." He spits at my feet. Lifting him off the ground, I lean the back out of the chair against the table. Spotting a cloth by the sink I throw the cloth over his mouth and nose.

Digging through the cabinets until I find a bucket, I fill it with water and walk over to him. Looking around, I spot the President who is leaning against the door frame with a smirk on his face. "Hold the motherfucker still."

He nods and grabs the man's shoulders. "You gonna talk, fucker?"

He shakes his head no. Lifting the bucket over his head, I start to pour the water over his nose and mouth slowly. He starts sputtering, coughing, and starts moving around trying to get away. A few seconds later, I pull the rag away from his mouth.

"Her fucking father is the one wanting her dead. I met her in college, and I've followed her since. My dad and her dad apparently knew each other. Waited forever for a chance to take what's mine, but your stupid ass cut right in. Her dad and me planned this all." He angrily tells me out of his toothless mouth. It's almost comical.

"Don't worry, her dad is fucking dead." Putting the rag back in his mouth, I take my gun out of my back pocket, but a hand on my arm stops me.

"Kill him, and we will put away the bodies. He won't be fucking found. We will throw his ass in a tub of acid and dump the rest of him in the lake out of the middle of the fucking woods." The President lets me go and steps back.

Putting the gun to his head, I pull the trigger not even thinking twice about it. Yeah killing someone is wrong, but I have a family to think about. I have a fiancée and kids. They're not going to be in danger again as long as I can help it. Putting some fucker down to keep them safe? Nothing to even contemplate.

I don't know the Prez of the MC Club, but I'm following my gut, and I know I can trust him. Turning around, I nod my head at him. Smacking him on the back, I say,

"Thanks, man."

"No thanks needed, man. I wanted these fuckers dead anyway. If it was my woman I would have done ten times worse."

Nodding my head, I walk out of the house without looking back. I have one thought and that thought is getting back to my woman.

nineteen

Sydney

Groaning, I roll over in bed. The bed feels hard and rough. The blanket covering me is stiff and doesn't hold any warmth. I start to shake from the cold, and I can feel my teeth chattering which causes my face to ache. *Where am I?*

Oh no. I'm still down in the basement. I raise up quickly and open my eyes while looking around frantically.

"Shhh, baby girl. I'm here, baby."

Warm hands touch my hand and arm. Looking over, I see Kane leaning over the bed—a worried expression on his face. Now that the blanket has fallen off me, the shaking and the cold is ten times worse.

Grabbing Kane's hand, I pull him, wanting him to get in bed with me. He starts to shake his head no. "Please,

Kane, I need this," I barely manage to get out through my chattering teeth.

He nods and kicks off his shoes. Climbing into bed, I lie on his chest. His arms wrap around me, and I'm surrounded by his warmth. I snuggle deeper as he pulls the covers over me with his arms around me. Down in the basement I felt like I would never get to see him or my kids again. I know Kane would do anything to find me, but so many things cross your mind in that situation.

Those guys were sick. Poor Emily. Her back and how they brutalized her body. No, it didn't happen to me, but I saw what her body looked like. That poor girl dated Cameron and when she found out what he was planning on doing to me, he did that to her and let his men have a go at her. Her back is a mess. Her whole entire back was marred with scars and that is something that will forever be engraved in my head.

"Sweetheart," Kane says while wiping away my tears. I never ever realized that I was crying. Taking my hand, I wipe my sore face. I wince when I hit the bruises.

"Did he?" he starts. He grips me tighter waiting for my answer.

Shaking my head furiously, he lets out a noticeable sigh of relief. I snuggle deeper into Kane wanting to crawl into him and forget the past two days. Then I notice the room around me and hear my babies' heartbeats.

"My babies. They're okay?" I ask Kane, scared.

"They're fine, baby." He kisses the top of my head and rubs his hand on my belly.

"Where are my kids?"

"They are with your mother." Nodding my head, I start to drift off. Being in Kane's arms makes me feel safe, and I just want to soak it up and revel in it.

Little voices wake me out of my sleep. Managing to open my sore and tired eyes, I notice Kane is still in bed with me. Looking around him I see Arabella and Carter staring at me scared.

"Momma huwt." Her bottom lip trembles.

Waving her forward, I raise up in bed and motion for Kane to pick her up. She sits on his lap and just stares at my face. "Mommy is okay, sweetheart."

She nods her little head. She then wraps her arms around my neck and climbs into my lap. I notice that Carter didn't come over. "You too, sweetheart."

He runs over and hugs my side. "I love you, Mom."

My heart is about to explode with joy. Tears roll down my face. "I love you too, Carter, so much." His little shoulders are shaking from crying. Kane looks at us all with a tortured look. He hates to see people cry.

"I love you," I mouth at him and he presses a kiss on my forehead.

"I love you, sweetheart. So much."

Closing my eyes, I smile because I have my family. Kane and these kids are my whole life. Kane popped into my life when I least expected it. Now I have my kids, Arabella and Carter, who captured mine and Kane's heart. Kissing the tops of their heads, I look up at Kane and smile.

Because of him, I have my forever and because of Kane protecting his forever, we now are a family.

epilogue

Six months later

I'm in labor. My water broke right in the middle of a restaurant. Kane left me standing because he lost his ever-loving mind when he saw that it was time. His face turned white as snow and his mouth fell open. He stared at my vagina like a baby was going to pop its head out and say peek-a-boo.

I carried these two babies to full-term which is rare for having twins. My boys didn't want to come into the world just yet. Yes, I'm having two little boys. God help me if they're anything like their dad.

Kane comes back a second later. He takes my hand and leads me out to his truck, his hand shaking as he does so. He opens the truck door and when he goes to lift me up I bend over as the first contraction hits. *Holy mother of God, that freaking hurts.*

"Oh shit, baby. Was that supposed to happen?" He starts wandering his hands all over my body like he can fix it and it freaking pisses me off.

"Get your hands off of me!" I hiss and glare at him.

He jumps back holding his hands up in the air. "Baby, I need to put you in the truck," he tries to convince me. Sighing, I lift my arms so he can pick me up.

Once my butt hits the soft leather seats I lean back to relax. Kane runs across the front of the vehicle and jumps in the truck. He puts the key in the ignition and burns rubber as he tries to race out of the parking lot.

"Holy mother of God!" I scream as another contraction hits. I grip my belly and bang my head against the window.

"This is killing me!" Kane yells and cusses at himself.

I can feel the horns sprouting out of my head. *"You!"* I scream. "I have a fucking head trying to squeeze its way out of my vagina. Which is fucking small!"

"I'm sorry!" he apologizes and tries to take my hand. I jerk my hand away glare at him.

"Keep your hands and demon dick away from me!" I yell and groan again as the contractions starts to fade.

Kane doesn't say anything else. Smart man. Then I feel bad, but I don't. "I'm sorry, Kane. It freaking hurts," I whine to him.

"I know, baby." He laughs and I see the bright lights of the hospital up ahead. Another contraction hits. I grab Kane's hand and bite a hunk out of it. *"Ouch!"* he yells and tries to pull away.

"That's nothing to what I'm feeling!" I yell at him again. He holds his injured hand and opens the truck door and runs inside to get a wheelchair, nurse, or whatever.

Five long hours later it's time for my baby boys to be born into the world. "Push!" The doctor yells at me. 9, 8, 7, the nurse counts down for the umpteenth time. Kane is holding my hand and the other is holding my leg back.

"You're doing good baby." Kane kisses my sweat-covered forehead.

"Here's its head!" One more push, the doctor tells me. Nodding, I give one more push. Then I can feel the baby leaving my body.

The nurse lays the baby on my belly and starts to cry. Laughing, I touch his little forehead. *God, he's beautiful.* Looking up at Kane I see tears falling down his face and the nurse takes the baby away to clean him up.

"All right, let's get ready for baby number two," the doctor says too cheerily.

"Okay," I grunt.

"So proud of you, Momma." Kane kisses my temple.

"Push," the doctor says and the nurse counts down.

Letting out a deep breath, I bite my lip at the pain. Tears run down my face. "One last time," the doctor tells me. Nodding my head once more I look around the room at my baby boy over across the room in the heater.

"Push," he tells me again. The nurse counts down again. Then I hear the cry of my second baby. She sets him down on my belly. I break out in sobs at the pure love I feel for these babies. They're finally here after these long months. I have four babies now.

Hours later the family leaves and it's just Kane, the babies, and me. Kane is holding both the babies against his chest with a content smile on his face. They both start to stir and whine. It's time for them to eat.

Kane stands up and lays one of the babies on my lap. Taking out my breast I grab the pillow and lay it under him. Elijah latches on. I run my finger across his chubby cheek.

"We make beautiful babies, sweetheart," Kane tells me in amazement as we look at these two little boys.

"Yes we do." I lean my head back so Kane can kiss me.

Fifteen years later.

"*Dad!* I'm about to kill Carter, Jacob, *and* Elijah!" Kane groans and takes his mouth away from mine. His fingers were up my pussy.

"I'm coming, Arabella." He sits back and gives me a wink. "I'm not done with you yet." Fixing my clothes, I follow after him.

Arabella is on the couch with her three brothers sitting on her back. Some other boy who is looking really nervous is sitting on the recliner a few feet away. I can see the wheels spinning in Kane's head from back here.

"Who are you?" Kane's voice booms through the house. Placing my hand over my mouth, I struggle to stifle the giggle. He leaves our sight for a second and comes back with a big ass shotgun.

"I-I-I-I'm Tommy," he stutters out and rubs his hands together.

"He asked me out on a date, Dad. I need you to get these *baboons* off of me!" She starts squirming all five foot nothing of herself. Carter just leans back and relaxes. All of my boys are over six foot. Carter is twenty-one, Arabella is seventeen, the boys are fourteen.

"You have a what? You really think I'm going to help you? You're too fucking young for that shit." He points at Arabella fuming. Then gives Tommy a pointed look.

She just shakes her head and laughs. She is used to hearing things like that. Her brothers nod their head in agreement.

"Daddy..." *Yeah, she said Daddy.* She is coming out with the big guns. A giggle escapes me and Kane glares at me. I hold my hands up—I'm taking no part in this.

"We're just going to the movies and then back home." She smiles at him sweetly. Carter chuckles.

"You're not going," he hisses and turns to glare at the boy who looks like he is about to shit his pants.

"Please, Daddy," she says in a sweet little girl voice. She has got that shit in the bag.

"Fine! Get her home at ten o'clock on the dot. Just know I'm cleaning my shotgun while you're gone, and I will be waiting outside for her." He glares down while pointing the shotgun at him. He gets right down in his face until they're almost nose to nose.

"Remember whatever you do to her I will do to you. Remember that as you try to get grabby. Plus, my daughter could kick your ass with one arm tied behind her back." He pats the boy on the shoulder who jumps out of his seat.

The boys let her up and they walk to the door together. Well, he is a good four feet away from her. He opens the door but stays far away. He practically runs out of the door. As soon as his vehicle starts up and pulls out of the driveway, Kane walks to the table and throws the boys his car keys and some money. "Follow his ass. I don't trust the fucker."

They smirk at their dad and go get their shoes on. I can't hold it in anymore. I bend over at the waist laughing. Kane is such a dad. Carter and the boys will follow her all night long. She won't even know. You know why? This isn't the first time this has happened.

The door slams closed, and then I'm airborne. Kane throws me over his shoulder and runs up the stairs. He throws me down on the bed and covers his body over mine. Sex with this man has gotten better over the years, there's no doubt about that.

My kids are growing up. Carter is a MMA fighter. Arabella can fight better than anyone I have ever seen. The boys are goof balls. The twins look just like Kane, but with my hair color. Handsome little devils and they know it.

My kids growing up is the worst thing ever. I remember the day I got Arabella and Carter. Then when I had my boys. Each and every day Kane showed me how much he loved me. I never once doubted the love he had for me. The kids are the center of our lives as they should be.

"I love you, Kane."

"I love you too, sweetheart."

acknowledgements

Mom, thank you for supporting me from the very beginning. Without you believing in me this book wouldn't have ever happened.

Johnna, you came into my life at the moment I needed you most. You started out as a PA and became one of my best friends. The person who tell me to suck it up when I curled into a ball and cried because I felt like my book was shit.

To my feedback ladies. You know who you are. I remember the first time I sent you a small bit of my book and you guys convinced me to write. I thought you guys were crazy considering I never wrote a day in my life prior. Without you guys pushing me I would gave up.

My sweethearts. I love you guys and thank you for all

your support.

A huge thank you to all the bloggers that shared my cover. I was astounded at all the shares. I want to thank you also for sharing about my release. <3

To my readers. Can't believe I can say that. I want to thank you for taking the time to read my debut. Which I spent months on. The one I laughed writing, cried, got mad and threw stuff across the room. Banged my head against the wall in frustration. But I did it for you guys. For my love of reading that turned into so much more!

Emma Mack, you swooped in at the very last moment and saved my butt. It's safe to say that I get to call you my friend. You put confidence back into me when I needed it the most. Love ya chick. <3

Another thank you to Sara Eirew my cover designer.

My promo lady Ena from enticing journey.

Without you guys this book wouldn't have ever happened. Thank you.

If you guys want to join my street team her is the link:

https://www.facebook.com/groups/982393471772249

Next comes Loving His Forever.
Braelyn and Ethan's epic story.

about the author

LeAnn Asher's is a blogger turned author who released her debut novel early 2016 and can't wait to see where this new adventure takes her. LeAnn writes about strong-minded females and strong protective males who love their women unconditionally.

More from LeAnn Ashers

Grim Sinners MC Series

Lane
Wilder
Forever Series

Protecting His Forever
Loving His Forever

Devil Souls MC Series

Torch
Techy
Butcher
Liam

Grim Sinners MC Series

Lane
Wilder

Made in the USA
Columbia, SC
11 February 2020

87798858R00135